HER PRETEND BILLIONAIRE BOYFRIEND

A CLEAN BILLIONAIRE ROMANCE BOOK ONE

BREE LIVINGSTON

Edited by

CHRISTINA SCHRUNK

Her Pretend Billionaire Boyfriend

Copyright © 2018 by **Bree Livingston**

Edited by Christina Schrunk

https://www.facebook.com/christinaschrunk.editor

Proofread by Krista R. Burdine

https://www.facebook.com/iamgrammaresque

Cover design by Victorine Lieske

http://victorinelieske.com/

Bree Livingston

https://www.breelivingston.com

Publisher's Note: This is a work of fiction. Names, characters, places, and incidents are a product of the author's imagination. Locales and public names are sometimes used for atmospheric purposes. Any resemblance to actual people, living or dead, or to businesses, companies, events, institutions, or locales is completely coincidental.

Her Pretend Billionaire Boyfriend / Bree Livingston. -- 1st ed.

ISBN: 9781983198717

I'd like to say thanks to Victorine Lieske for putting up with all my questions, breakouts, odd moods, weird sense of humor and for being a genuinely kind person.

I'd like to thank my editor, Christina Schrunk for taking a book that looked like burnt toast and turning into yummy cinnamon sugar toast.

I'd also like to thank my beta readers Audrey Rich, Maria Molina, Rachel John, and I know I'm forgetting someone. I now because...squirrel.

CHAPTER 1

Tristan Stone swiveled his chair away from the boardroom table and looked out over the Seattle skyline. The sun glinted off the windows of the Space Needle while a white-capped Mount Rainier stood in the background. He wished he was there, on the top of the mountain, and not dwelling on the board meeting that had just ended. He didn't want to think about the dozen or so men and women who'd argued about which direction his grandmother would've wanted him to take the cruise line he'd inherited.

He missed her.

Find someone to love, sweetheart. Not all women will want you for your money. His grandmother's words resounded like a megaphone in his head. He could still feel the aged hand touching his cheek and see the wrinkled face smiling up at him. Even while she was sick, she'd been thinking of him.

He'd tried to convince her he didn't feel lonely, but she could always see through him. Three months, and not a day went by that he didn't miss her laughter and wisdom.

"Tristan!" Grayson Matthews's voice broke through his thoughts. "Are you listening to me?"

"No," he said without taking his eyes off the skyline.

"Nice. Real nice." Grayson huffed, pulling a chair directly in front of him and sitting backward in it.

Tristan leveled his eyes at him. "What?"

"That board meeting was out of control. Why didn't you do anything?"

Why? Because he didn't want to do anything. His grandmother wasn't even cold, and vultures were circling. "My head isn't here." He had tasks to finish for his grandma. One of which was taking a cruise on the last ship she'd designed so he could spread her ashes over the ocean.

Grayson's icy blue eyes softened. "Buddy, I know you miss her, but if you want this company to continue, you're going to have to bring that alpha dog reputation you've created to the table."

Alpha dog. Tristan snorted. "I know, but this is different. I'm not buying up a company. This was *her* company. A company...people...I promised to take care of." He was used to taking over companies, bull-dozing over anything that got in the way of making it successful and turning it into a thriving business. This was different. He'd made a solemn vow to take care of her employees, among other things. Things he wasn't willing to tell his best friend.

"Listen, man, I know you were close to her, but..."

Tristan stood and raked a hand through his dark-brown hair. "I am not selling this company. I'll buy out everyone's shares if I have to. I don't care if I go bank-rupt keeping it." He closed his eyes. He wasn't just close to his grandmother. Other than Grayson and his Aunt Felicia, she was the only person he trusted to love him for more than his money.

The chair squeaked as Grayson stood. "Maybe you should take a vacation. Get out of here, get some fresh air, grieve. Come back when you're ready to make some hard decisions."

Grayson continued when he didn't respond. "Seri-ously, take one. Two weeks. What can possibly happen in two weeks without you here? It's been three months, and nothing's changed yet." Grayson grasped his shoulder and turned him around. "You took care of her the last eight months of her life. I know it had to be hard on you. Taking a break will help."

Tristan did like the idea. The stress of taking care of a loved one was worse than he ever imagined. The last month or so, his grandma didn't even know who he was. She'd look at him with a blank expression most of the time, and when she was even remotely coherent, she'd call him by his father's name, Thomas.

He *had* promised his grandma that he'd take a cruise and spread her ashes. May as well get it done. He could check that off the list. "Maybe you're right."

Grayson smiled and pulled out his phone. "Ohhh, I'm going to need you to say that again. I want to record it and replay it when you're being arrogant and egotistical."

"I'm not arrogant or egotistical. I'm just right all the time." Tristan chuckled.

His friend's eyes widened. "Let me take care of it. I've got the perfect place in mind. Hot women, warm sand, cool clear water. I can even picture it. The two of us, lounging next to some tropical oasis and sipping fruity drinks that come in pineapples." He pulled up the search engine on his phone. "Cheesy, but tasty."

Tristan rubbed his knuckles down his jaw. "No, I want to go somewhere no one will recognize me. I want to be left alone." He wanted to be Tristan. Not

Tristan Stone the billionaire. He wanted to feel normal. For once, he wanted to be just one of the guys. An idea began to form.

"You might try Mars, then. You're a thirty-one-year-old billionaire, and you're in every socialite paper known to man. And with that baby face of yours? Good luck." Grayson laughed.

"I could grow a beard." The words popped out of Tristan's mouth. What? He hated beards. They were itchy.

Grayson lifted an eyebrow. "You? Dude, you tried that, remember? A five o'clock shadow nearly had you in a straightjacket."

That was true, but if it could give him some anonymity, maybe it was worth it. "I'll try again." And if he went undercover on the cruise ship, maybe he could get a better understanding of the company.

"Okay, if you think you can." Grayson's lack of confidence didn't help.

Tristan tugged on his dark-gray suit coat, straightening it. "And I want to go alone. I think I need it."

His best friend's face fell. "What? But I'm your wingman, your right-hand dude, your mate, your—"

"I know. Normally, I'd want you to come, but I really think I need some time alone." Plus, he didn't want Grayson to know what he was really planning.

Grayson eyed him and then huffed. "Fine, but you owe me a paradise getaway with hot women."

"Aren't you dating that model? What's her name?" Tristan wracked his brain. Grayson had a new girlfriend every five seconds. "Gwen Hanover."

He shrugged and looked at the floor. "Nah, she was okay, but she had this weird thing where she smacked her gum."

"You broke it off because she smacked her gum? I met her twice. Neither time was she chewing gum." He'd never met a guy so afraid of commitment.

"Yeah."

Tristan shook his head. "One of these days, you're going to have to evaluate a woman on more than her quirks. Granted, I didn't think she was good for you, but she wasn't horrible either. Not nearly as bad as that Heather woman."

Grayson grunted and shivered. "At least I date."

"I date. I date a lot." Tristan was also lonely. A lot. The women who were attracted to him were typically interested in two things: his money or their fifteen minutes of fame from being associated with him. It happened enough times that he'd stopped asking anyone out.

A thin dark eyebrow went up, and Grayson pierced him with a look.

Tristan shook his head. "Fine, so I don't. I have to go. I've got some plans to make."

"Okay, but don't forget, you owe me." His friend pointed a finger at him.

"Whatever." Tristan grinned and walked out of the room. He needed a beard, a single room, and passage on a cruise ship.

BELLE EVANS'S leg bounced as she waited to board the cruise ship. Never in her wildest dreams would she have thought she'd win a cruise and ten grand. All her life, she'd figured those contests were hoaxes. Who sticks their name in a box and actually thinks they're going to win something? She'd hung up on the radio guy twice before he'd convinced her she'd won.

She wasn't the only winner, either. At least twenty others had won, or that's what she was told by the cruise people when she got her tickets. They'd be picking out random paying passengers too. Something about fixing their image and using them as advertisement by getting photos and feedback at the end of the cruise. If it weren't for the ten grand that came with the trip, she wouldn't be going. It'd given her the ability to get ahead on her mom's nursing home payments.

Her phone buzzed, and she checked it. Ugh. Laura, her best friend since high school who was now her ex-best friend, had been calling incessantly all morning. How many times was she going to call? She needed to catch a clue and leave her alone.

Their relationship had always been like that. Laura would do something to hurt her, and for some reason, Belle would always forgive her. This was different. She'd done something that Belle couldn't just brush off this time. It was time to stop thinking about Laura and get on with her cruise.

Over the last hour, other passengers had arrived one by one, and now the most gorgeous man she'd ever seen was standing about a foot behind her. His dark, wavy hair was neat except for a cute little wild piece curling over his ear. He had dazzling dark-brown eyes. She only knew that because he'd caught her staring earlier. The smile he'd shot her almost made her fall to the floor.

It had reminded her of another smile, and she'd worked to avoid looking in his direction again. She didn't need any complications, and a man would definitely be a complication.

"Nervous?" he asked.

She startled. "What?"

He pointed to her foot. It was tapping so fast her nickname could have been Thumper.

Her cheeks heated up, and she hooked her foot around her other leg. "No, I'm just fidgety. I'm not used to just standing and waiting."

His smile was warm. Not flirty, but genuine. "Well, no worries about that. You're going to be doing a lot of running on the cruise. From what I understand, there's a lot to do." He scratched the little more than a five o'clock shadow growing on his jaw.

"I know. Guess it's not the worst thing in the world to be forced to relax." She twisted a piece of her strawberry blonde hair around her finger. "Is your beard new?"

He lifted his head, and again his brown eyes found hers. "What?"

She touched her jaw. "Your beard? Is it new? I'm only asking because you keep scratching it."

The man jerked his hand away from his face. "Oh, yeah, I'm just trying something different. Everyone tells me I have a baby face, and I'm tired of it."

It did look good on him, but she tried picturing him without it. "I like it. It makes you look distinguished."

Before he said another word, he quickly closed the

gap between them. "I thought distinguished is what young people called old men."

Oh, good lord, he was a tower of a man. Olive skin, broad shoulders, thickly built, soulful brown eyes, and he smelled like spice. Butterflies met the tingles flooding her body, and they danced the rumba all over her. "Uh, well, it could apply to anyone. I mean, the definition means successful, authoritative, and commanding respect. I don't think you have to be old to do that." Did her voice squeak? She cleared her throat, just in case.

"Name's Tristan. What's yours?" This time, she noticed his deep baritone voice. It was like rich espresso. The kind that's smooth and potent.

He stuck a hand out, and as she shook it, she said, "Belle, Belle Evans." Her mom had loved literature, and she'd given her the same love. Belle just wished her mom could remember it.

His eyebrows shot up. "Like *Twilight*?"

She rolled her eyes. "No, Belle as in *Beauty and the Beast*."

"Oh, right. I tend to get those two mixed up." He rubbed the back of his neck. "I'm sorry."

"It's okay. So, did you win too?" Not that she needed to know, she just wanted to keep him talking because she liked the sound of his voice.

Something she couldn't put a finger on flashed across his features. "No, I bought my ticket. You won?"

"Yeah, I never expected to win. It was a whim. I'd forgotten I even entered. That radio guy sounded frustrated with me, but I did hang up on him twice." Her phone vibrated, and she looked down at it. Again? With a huff, she pressed the decline-call button.

Tristan smiled at her again. "Problem?"

Belle leaned over to see where she was in line. It resembled an airport terminal with a long counter and agents behind computers checking people in. The person in front of her moved ahead, and she stepped forward, pulling her luggage behind her.

She wanted to tell him, "Yep, my best friend stealing my fiancé was a huge problem," but instead, she pasted on a smile and shook her head. "No. I just want to be able to concentrate on what I'm doing." At least on the cruise, Belle wouldn't be dealing with Laura calling her all the time.

"Good idea." He caught her gaze and held it. "You have really pretty eyes."

Belle's fascination with Tristan screeched to a halt. The one thing she didn't want was a relationship or fling or anything else while she was on a nine-day cruise. And if both of them were going to be on the same ship, they'd definitely have the opportunity to spend time together. "Thanks." She turned her back on him, unwilling to take the chance of being burned again.

The line moved again, and Belle got a little closer to the woman in front of her. Hopefully, that'd give Mr. Smooth Voice a hint she wasn't interested. Her jackhammering heart needed to cut it out. Falling for someone wasn't on the to-do list. She just needed to get on board and forget her troubles, like Paul getting her fired.

It was stupid. Paul was the one who chased her. Paul was the one who asked her out and then asked her to marry him. It was all Paul Whitlock. The snake. He'd fed her so many lies, and she'd eaten them up like pie at a church picnic. Then he'd sabotaged her marketing campaign, cheated on her with her best friend, and dumped her. A whole year of blood, sweat, and tears to build her fledgling marketing career, gone straight down the drain.

Finally, it was her turn to check in. She had to answer several questions, like whether she'd been sick recently, and have her debit card tied to her room card so she could make purchases, which she had no intention of doing.

Once all her paperwork was in order, she got her room card and made her way toward the deck of the ship. As she turned away from the ticket counter, she glanced at Tristan. His dark eyes followed her the entire way, and whatever he was thinking was a mystery. The man could obviously play poker.

A woman in a cruise uniform smiled as Belle stopped at the entrance to the ship. "Hello, welcome aboard. We'll be leaving port tonight. We hope you'll have a wonderful time. If there is anything you need, please ask. Crew and staff can be identified with neck lanyards and uniforms."

"Okay, thank you." Belle let her gaze sweep across the ship. It was massive and modern, making the one she'd worked on look small and dated.

"Since you're a contest winner, we'd like to have you meet in the dining hall as part of the marketing you agreed to when you accepted the ticket. If you have any additional questions, someone will be able to answer them."

"Oh, okay. Thanks. I'm just excited to get a vacation." Belle smiled.

The woman smiled wider, if that was possible. "That's what we like to hear. An excited passenger having a good time."

CHAPTER 2

*A*fter unpacking, Tristan sat on the full-size bed in his standard interior room aboard the ship. He was used to plush, spacious suites. It was okay —obviously not as big as his penthouse—but he could handle anything for a week. One thing his grandmother taught him was that nothing lasts forever. It was true for almost everything. Although, loneliness seemed to be lasting forever. He'd promised her he'd find someone, but she didn't understand how hard it was.

Once women found out he was billionaire Tristan Stone, they changed. They no longer saw him as a person, just a means to an end. If he could find someone who loved him, truly loved him, he'd jump at the chance to make it work.

He immediately thought of Belle Evans. He'd thought about her spectacular smile and dark-green eyes since he'd seen her. When he first caught her staring, he thought his cover was blown. After talking to her though, he was certain she had no clue. He'd complimented her on her eyes and caught himself before he went further. Good thing too. Telling her she had beautiful eyes turned her icy so fast she could've been liquid nitrogen. Which was a good thing. He *needed* to put her out of his mind and concentrate on being a regular passenger. The point of the trip was to check out the ship and get away. Not get involved.

He raked his hand through his hair before rubbing his hands on his jeans and standing. A walk around the ship would be good to get his mind off everything. It couldn't hurt to go ahead and get a feel for the ship. As he stepped out of his room, a body bounced off his back.

A familiar scent of coconut and flowers floated around him. "Oh, sorry!"

He turned, and her large green eyes lifted to his face. A nervous excitement bloomed in the pit of his stomach. "Belle, right?" As if he could forget her name.

They eyed a couple of other passengers and waited for them to enter their rooms.

Belle smiled. "Uh, yeah. Your room is right next to mine?"

"Yeah. It seems so."

Tristan wanted more time with her. He might not be interested in a relationship, but he wouldn't mind a little company while he was on the cruise. "I was about to go exploring. Would you want to come with me? I figured it couldn't hurt to get a lay of the land, or ship in this case."

Belle chewed her bottom lip for a second, like she was debating. "Uh, I don't know. I've got this marketing thing I have to attend in a little while."

"You do? I was randomly chosen for that."

Her little eyebrows went up. "You were?"

"Yeah, they said they'd give me a reduced fare if I participated." He paused. "So, exploring with me?"

For a heartbeat, she let the question hang in the air like she wasn't sure if she wanted to or not. Then she said, "Sure. Why not?"

"Great." He hadn't meant to sound so enthusiastic. "I mean, good. I'd hate to wander around alone."

"So, where to first?"

"I don't know. Where do you want to go?" Tristan was curious where she'd pick. He figured she'd say the stores or something like that, like most of the women he dated.

"How about the top deck?" She glanced up at him.

He grinned. "Sounds like a good idea."

"I never expected to win something like this. Have you ever won anything crazy like this?" she asked as they walked the hall, passing other passengers arriving.

Tristan shook his head. "No."

Her pouty lips parted with a smile. "I'm surprised your room's next to mine."

They reached the elevator and stepped inside.

"I am too, but it's a good surprise." He returned her smile.

The elevator continued up, and the moments ticked by before she said, "Yeah, I think so too. I was a little nervous about coming by myself, but I couldn't pass up the trip."

"My grandmother loved cruises and the ocean. She said breathing salt air was akin to cleaning out a closet. You breathe it in, and when you let it out, you let all your clutter go with it." He startled, not meaning to bring up his grandmother.

"Loved? Past tense?" she asked.

Tristan nodded. She was perceptive. The loss still caused his chest to tighten. "I lost her three months ago. I still miss her."

Belle placed her hand on his bicep, and her touch

sent tingles through his shoulder. "I'm sorry. I kinda know what that's like."

For a heartbeat, his mouth wouldn't work. "Thanks."

The elevator dinged, and the doors opened. He was glad the ship was docked in Miami. Even in May, Seattle would have been chilly. In sunny Florida, the temperature was perfect. "Looks like our stop."

She stepped out first, and he joined her on the top deck. Even though they were still docked, the side they stood on was open to the water. Seagulls squawked and floated on the breeze.

Taking a deep breath, Belle gripped the railing and leaned back. "This is going to be nice. This ship is relatively new, and from the research I've done, the previous owner, billionaire Beverly Richmond, personally helped with the design not long before she died."

Of course, Tristan knew that. He'd been away with his own business dealings, but when his grandmother called, she'd tell him all about her new cruise ship. "I heard that too. She has a grandson, doesn't she?"

Belle shrugged. "I don't know. I just wanted information on the ship, and there was a little paragraph about her designing it. Laura, a friend I used to be close to, would know. She keeps up with all that society, gossip junk. If she did have a grandson, I bet he's brokenhearted, and I think people should leave him alone."

Tristan nodded. He couldn't remember the last time he'd met a woman who cared about someone other than herself. "I think so too. Have you ever been on a cruise before?"

"I worked on a cruise ship that sailed out of Louisiana. It was awful. It was old, moldy, and leaky." She scrunched up her face. "I only stuck with it so I could finish my masters in marketing." Her eyes grew large. "I'd prefer if no one knew that."

BELLE WANTED TO KICK HERSELF. She'd already over-shared. Why couldn't she keep her big mouth shut? He didn't need to know she had a masters in marketing. That would only lead to questions, and the answers were something she didn't want to share.

"What do you do for a living?" she asked.

For a moment, she thought he would press her, but he dropped his arms and turned his face into the breeze. "A little bit of this, a little bit of that. I was a bit transient, you could say, until I settled in Seattle."

Transient? Like homeless? Poor guy. Maybe he just

liked moving. She wouldn't ask in case it was a sensitive subject. "Oh, what was that like? I've lived a few places, but I wouldn't call myself transient."

"Where?" He seemed genuinely interested.

"Let's see. I've lived in New York, Boston, Dallas, and now I live here in Miami. How about you?" She needed the focus to stay on him, even though it seemed like he was trying to turn it back on her every chance he got.

He shrugged and looked down. "Oh, here and there. I lived in Houston until I was ten. Then I moved to Seattle. Once I finished school, I decided I wanted to see the world."

"Seattle seems like a pretty city. I haven't been there yet. I've always meant to go, but things got in the way." Things like Paul Whitlock.

The smile he turned on her made her grip the railing harder, and her heart stuttered. It was her weak point. A great smile got her every time, and Tristan's was the best she'd ever seen.

"You'll have to look me up if you ever do. I can show you around. I know all the great spots to see."

The alphabet floated in her mind, and words tried to form. "Uh." That's all she could come up with? Uh? What was her problem? He was attractive, sure, but it wasn't like she'd never been around a good-looking man before. Mentally, she smacked herself. If she could've physically done it without looking like a freak, she would have. "That would be nice."

"I think I could stand here all day, but I guess we should actually explore, huh?" A small dimple appeared as one corner of his lips quirked up. She hadn't noticed that before.

Belle dragged her gaze from his dimple to his eyes. "I suppose so."

Maybe moving would keep her brain from seizing and she could have a conversation with him. She pushed off the railing and walked next to him down the deck. Being next to him made her feel like a doll. "So, you said you're transient. Have you been to the Caribbean before?"

"A few times, but I don't think you can ever visit it too many times. It's beautiful. I love snorkeling." He raked a hand through his hair, and the wind picked up a few pieces, making them take funny shapes. It made her want to run her fingers through it and smooth them out.

"What?" he asked.

She blinked. "What?"

"You're looking at me funny. Do I have something on my face?" His dark eyes held hers, and it was at least three heartbeats before she took a breath.

No, there was nothing on his beautiful face. She only wanted to run her hands through his hair because it was all wild, and she bet it felt great. Cripes. That was not the correct answer, even though it was the truth. This guy was pressing every button she had, and it was only the first day. "Oh, uh, no. Your hair is just kinda sticking up in places."

He raked his hand through it again. "Is that better?"

A giggle escaped, despite her fight to keep it in. "No." It was worse, but she wouldn't say that.

They passed a chair, and she stepped onto the seat. She grabbed his arm and stood him in front of her. His hair was as silky as she thought it'd be as she ran her fingers through it, trying to fix the wayward strands. "I'm not sure it'll matter with the way the wind is blowing."

"How tall are you?" he asked.

She flicked her gaze to his and lifted an eyebrow. "Not that short." Tristan stood at least a foot taller than her, but she'd always been drawn to tall men.

He rolled his eyes. "Seriously."

She put her hands on her hips. "I'm five feet one and one-quarter inch."

"That quarter inch is important, huh?" His lips quirked up, and his teeth showed through. It was an award-winning smile. Not as good as the sexy half-smile, but still great.

Belle grinned. "Absolutely."

She finished fixing his hair and looked at him. "There."

"All good?" The corners of his eyes creased as his smile reached them.

Then she realized just how close he was and how great he smelled. Good gravy, he smelled fantastic. Spice and sea air mixed and rolled around her. Her mouth went dry. "Um, yeah, all good." She jumped down before any other temptations popped up. Tristan wasn't just good looking; he gave her this feeling of comfort and safety. He was someone she could see herself falling for. Those thoughts needed to stop. She wasn't on the cruise to find a man. It was to refresh and regroup. That's it.

"Thanks." He remained still as he looked down at her.

He was so close that if he was threatening at all, she would call it looming. She didn't get that vibe from him though. He struck her as the large teddy-bear type. The kind you cuddled with on the couch, eating popcorn and watching movies. Tingles erupted just thinking about it. Yeah, she needed to put at least a foot between them. A ruler might be necessary.

After that, Belle concentrated on keeping her distance and watching what she said. They explored the ship for hours before returning to their rooms to freshen up before they were supposed to do the marketing thing. Knowing Tristan was in the room next to hers made her heart trip. She'd be seeing him every day. If she didn't get a grip, she'd end up making a fool of herself.

CHAPTER 3

*B*elle blew out a long breath and entered the expansive dining hall. She discreetly glanced around the room. About a dozen people were already seated, and more were filing in. Hopefully, whatever it was they were supposed to be doing would be over quickly.

Her gaze landed on Tristan and the group of women surrounding him. Jade-green jealousy nearly smothered her, and she pushed it down. There was no reason to be jealous. They were just friends, if that. They'd just met. Acquaintances was the better word, and she wasn't looking for a relationship. What did she care if he was flocked by women?

Tristan lifted his head and smiled.

Her lips curved up like they had a mind of their

own, and butterflies fluttered in her stomach. Ugh. Her body needed to stop.

He stood and walked to her. "Hey, I saved you a seat if you want to sit over there."

Getting to know some of the other people on board wouldn't be bad. "Sure."

His palm came to rest on the small of her back as they walked, and warmth spread through her. "Those women seem friendly enough, but they don't understand personal space."

Belle nearly choked, trying to keep from snorting. Those women understood personal space just fine. They'd deliberately invaded his personal space. She couldn't fathom him not seeing that. As they approached, the ladies sat back and looked her up and down. It took effort not to roll her eyes. If they wanted Tristan, they could have him.

"Hi," she said and stuck out her hand. There was no point in starting the cruise on bad terms with any of the other winners. "I'm Belle Evans."

A platinum blonde with a short reverse bob shook her hand and smiled sweetly. "I'm Ashley Parks."

"I'm Maritsa Ara." The other one had a light Cuban accent, long dark hair, and expressive dark eyes. "It's nice to meet you."

"It's nice to meet you. I think I remember seeing

you earlier today." Belle took her seat and placed her hands in her lap.

Tristan sat next to her and leaned in her direction. "I guess I was in my own world."

Ashley batted his arm. "Just like a guy."

"Yeah, I guess so." He wasn't hiding his discomfort well.

Belle looked over her shoulder, and an average-height man with sandy blonde hair walked in. He had clean-shaven face with bright-blue eyes. Maritsa waved him over.

He beamed as he took a seat next to Maritsa. "Hi, I'm Shawn Miller."

One by one, they introduced themselves and chatted until a slim middle-aged woman stood at the front of the room. "I'm Felicia Fredricks. I'll be your passenger liaison during the voyage. There are a few things we need to go over, and then we'll take a tour of the ship."

Tristan jerked his head up to look at the woman speaking.

At the same time, Ashley leaned over and said, "I heard she was good friends with the owner, Beverly Richmond."

Tristan swung his gaze to Ashley, and Belle could swear he looked pained.

She leaned over to him and touched his arm. "Are you okay?"

He nodded and smiled, but it didn't look genuine. "Yeah."

Belle had seen that look before. He wasn't telling the truth. He was just another hot guy with something to hide. "Okay." She forced herself to sound nonchalant.

Once Felicia was done going over expectations— like leisure time, schedules, and the requirement of giving their opinion of the cruise when they docked back in Miami—she invited them to follow her around the ship. Touring earlier with Tristan had been nice, but she was glad they were doing it again. The ship was huge, and she'd already forgotten how to get to some of the places they'd visited.

"I think I may have to get myself a map," Tristan leaned down and whispered.

Belle's skin prickled everywhere his breath touched. But he was a liar. "Yeah." Why was she so disappointed? Wasn't it a good thing she figured it out early on?

He touched her arm. "Are you okay?"

It was like a lit match being held against her skin. She flinched away. "I'm fine. It's been a long day. I'm ready to get some sleep."

Maritsa turned. "Oh no, we're going to play a little pool after this. Get to know one another."

I don't want to, flitted through her mind, but what came out of her lips was, "I really can't."

"Come on," Ashley said as she walked on the other side of Shawn. "It'll just be the five of us. I heard the other winners saying they were going to be hitting the slides."

Belle didn't want to be the ship's official party pooper, so she relented. "Fine."

"Awesome," Shawn said, and Belle noticed him lightly holding Maritsa's hand. A cruise ship connection had already been made, apparently.

Tristan shot her a half-smile, his little dimple showing, but he didn't say anything.

So what if he was going to be there. She could be an adult. She could handle the hot guy with the lying tongue. "I have to warn you, though, I stink at pool. Like, you'd better duck if I'm hitting the white ball."

"You mean breaking?" Ashley asked with a snicker.

Belle chuckled. "Whatever it's called. Anytime I hit the ball, the white one takes flight. People who know me fear me."

"I can teach you," Tristan said. "I was pretty good in college."

She didn't want him near her. "That's okay. It's not

a skill I care to master." It had come out harsher than she'd planned. The second he touched her arm, the mood turned uncomfortable.

"Could you guys give us a second?" Tristan asked the group.

"Sure," Shawn said as he eyed them.

Tristan waited until the three of them were well out of earshot. "Did I do something to upset you? If I did, I'm truly sorry."

"I'm fine. We should catch back up." Belle didn't want to give him a chance to lie anymore.

His shoulders rounded, and his eyebrows knitted together. "Please, tell me."

She hesitated. What did it matter? He'd just lie some more. Paul had taught her that. With a huff, she said, "Fine. You lied when I asked if you were okay. I think you know Felicia Fredericks." At least she'd know if he was a habitual liar.

He sank down into a chair sitting on the deck. "She reminded me of my grandma."

Belle squeezed her eyes shut and tried to forcibly remove the foot she'd put in her mouth. She pulled a chair next to his. "I'm so sorry. I should have known it was something like that."

"I just didn't want to talk about it with all those people there. It's not something I want everyone to know." He looked up, and his eyes held so much sorrow it nearly broke her heart.

She was such an idiot. Of course it was something like that. Not every guy was a liar like Paul. "I'm so sorry. Do you want to talk about it now?"

"There's really not much to talk about. We took a cruise like this when I was a little boy. So much of it reminds me of her. It makes it hard. I know three months should be enough time to get over it, but she was my best friend. I loved her." His voice broke, and Belle couldn't stop herself from hugging him.

His arms circled around her, and he held her tightly. "People assume because I'm this big guy that things like loss should just roll right off of me, but they don't."

"You're allowed to grieve for your grandma as long as you want. You're allowed to be angry, confused, and sad. There are no rules for losing someone."

She leaned back, and her breath caught as she saw tears clinging to his lashes. "And anyone who tries to mess with you will have to go through me, okay?" She'd never wanted to soothe someone's ache as much as she wanted to soothe his. It had always been like that with her. She hated seeing someone hurting.

His lips turned up in a partial smile, but the sadness clung to him. "Thanks."

Belle let him go and set her hands in her lap. "We should probably catch up to the group. I need time to create some bullseyes for later when I'm playing pool. I figure I'll just hang them around everyone's neck, and I'll keep score like that." She'd give anything to see him smile or hear him laugh.

Tristan chuckled, and her heart skipped a beat. "You're really that bad?"

"Horrible. There should be actual laws that prohibit me from playing." She winked at him, took his hand, and pulled him out of the chair.

She let go of his hand, but he reached for it again and held it. "Thanks for that, really. Most people just tell me to shake it off. They don't really see or hear me."

Before she could think it through, she reached up and cupped his cheek. "They must not know grief. It's not something you can just shake off. I see you, and I hear you." The intimacy of the moment shook her to the core. She thought Paul had obliterated any chance of feeling that way toward someone, but there was something different about Tristan. He was innately good. That is, if she could trust her gut instinct.

Belle pulled her hand back and grinned at him sheepishly. "Sorry. Um, we should go."

Tristan nodded. "Yeah." The word was so soft she almost didn't hear it.

Man, he was sweet. Paul had been sweet in the beginning too. This was only the first day. Anyone could be anything for a day. She needed to keep her head on her shoulders and her feet on the ground. Tristan was just someone to talk to, nothing more.

WITH A GRUNT, Tristan sat up, scrubbing his face with his hands, and stood. It was the middle of the night, and he'd yet to fall asleep. He'd come on this cruise to get away, to have time alone. Instead, he was following Belle Evans around like a puppy. She'd been kind to him. More kind than anyone had in a long time. It was almost like she understood. It made him wonder if she'd lost someone.

He was going to have to watch himself around Belle. She was incredibly perceptive, and she caught things most people didn't. Another thing he liked about her. His cheek still tingled where she'd touched him. It's been a sweet gesture. She said she'd seen him and heard him. No one had ever said that before. He shook his head. That's not why he'd come on the cruise. Belle was just a friend, if that. They'd just met.

It seemed like it was in her nature to be kind, and he didn't need to be reading into it or letting his thoughts wander anywhere else.

His Aunt Felicia was on board. He had no idea she'd be on this boat. She'd seen him, he was sure of that, but she'd let him keep his anonymity. She must have known if he was sitting in a marketing group, he was wanting to keep his identity a secret. Of course, he was sure he'd get a call to the office at some point. He hadn't seen her since the funeral, and they were pretty close.

Thinking about his aunt reminded him of how quickly Belle had pushed him away after he hadn't been honest with her. He was so torn. If she hated being lied to about such a small thing, he couldn't imagine how upset she would be if she found out his whole identity was a lie. She must have gone through something terrible to be so quick to see he wasn't being honest. She could probably sniff out a lie a mile away.

Should he tell her who he was or not? If he didn't tell her and she found out, she'd probably be completely done with him. If he did tell her and it changed her, he'd hate himself. What if he trusted her and she betrayed him by telling everyone? He didn't get that vibe from her, but he didn't know her well enough to really judge.

He rubbed his palm against his forehead. He couldn't tell her yet, even if it meant she would hate him later. The anonymity was freeing, and he wasn't ready to give it up yet. He liked being just Tristan to her, to all of them.

It has been so much fun to play pool with Amber, Shawn, Maritsa, and Belle. Shawn reminded him of a surfer he followed. He didn't ask him about it because there was a good chance he was doing the same thing as Tristan and keeping his identity a secret.

They saw him as just a guy, and it was nice to be treated like a regular person. Not once did he see dollar signs in their eyes. Belle hadn't lied about her inability to play pool, either. She'd nearly clocked Maritsa before putting down the pool cue and giving up. There was an audible collective sigh of relief when she did.

He'd needed today. It'd given him a moment to forget his grief and enjoy life. He felt like his grandmother was still taking care of him. Like when she asked him to take the cruise, she knew he'd try to blend with the crowd. In her last few months, when she still recognized him, they'd talked a lot about her final wishes.

The role of caretaker had always fallen to him, even when he was little. He'd been the one covering his parents with blankets because they'd fallen asleep after working too late. After they died and he was sent to live with his grandmother, he worked to take care of her too. She didn't seem to expect it, but he felt she was owed for having to raise another child.

Exhaling sharply, he sat down hard on the bed. His little excursion as just Tristan was turning out to be more than the simple little adventure he wanted. He stretched out on the bed and crossed his arms under his head. His thoughts ran back to Belle.

What was it about her, anyway? He barely knew her. It wasn't just her, though, if he was honest. He was tired of being alone. For the last few years, he'd focused solely on taking the reins of his late father's investment firm, and then he'd started his own company. Then he'd concentrated on his grandmother when her health began to decline.

Tristan, my sweet boy, life is about more than business. You are such a good boy, and I love you for taking care of me. You need to take care of you, too. Find a girl and settle down. Promise me this, Tristan. Promise me.

Balance. He needed balance. He just wasn't sure how to do it.

CHAPTER 4

Belle finished applying her makeup and studied herself in the mirror. She'd chosen pale-green palazzo pants, an off-the-shoulder flowy white blouse, and a wrap for her first full cruise day. The outfit brought out her eyes and complemented her fair skin. And the sweater would keep her warm. She was always cold. Enough that most people thought she was crazy.

With one last look in the mirror, she went to the door. As she stepped through, Tristan stepped out of his. His scent curled around her. How did he always smell so good? He looked good, too, in his dark-gray slacks and dark-blue dress shirt.

"Hi," he said as he walked her way.

"Hey. You ready for your first day of being at sea?"

she asked, discreetly wiping her hands down her pants. Why were her palms suddenly sweaty? Good grief.

Tristan shot her a smile and nodded. "I am. Are you?"

Had he figured out she liked that smile? The sexy, flirty half-smile. "I think so. I'm always nervous on the first day of anything." She pulled her gaze away from his smile and mentally chastised herself. He could smile like he was blessed by heaven, but she wasn't interested in a relationship. He was a nice man and easy to talk to. That was it. She was an adult. She could have a friendship with a man.

"You look fantastic." He reached out like he was about to touch her hair but jerked his hand back. "Well, you ready to go relax and cruise?"

"Uh, yeah, I sure am." She clasped her hands in front of her as they walked to the elevator. "Are you going to be hanging around in Miami after the cruise is over?" Why did she ask that? She wanted to thump herself in the forehead.

"I hadn't thought about it. You live there, right?" He pressed the up arrow for the elevator.

For the last six months she had. Maybe by the end of the cruise, enough time would have passed that she could start her marketing career over. "Yeah, I do."

The elevator doors opened, and they got in. "Maybe I'll consider it."

"Will your job miss you?"

Tristan grinned. "I was due a vacation and have a little leeway. I wasn't sure I'd be ready to go back after the cruise, so I left it open."

"Well, I guess I'll have to make sure you want to hang around."

Why did she say that? Her cheeks heated as he smiled. Why was she flirting with him? It's like her brain stopped working when she was around him. Her head screamed, "Remember Paul!" Her heart did a silly dance and cooed. Stupid heart.

He stepped closer. "Is that so?"

Her lips parted. How could she be so attracted to someone she just met? Someone she didn't even know? He could be a weirdo or something. She didn't get that vibe, but her track record wasn't exactly stellar when it came to instinct about a guy. Her galloping heart needed to cut it out.

Paul Whitlock was good-looking with a great smile. They'd dated six months. She was head over heels for him, but then they'd competed for the same account. He'd used mind games and twisted everyone against her, including her best friend. Her heart had been so broken. She'd slowly gotten over it, but it made her cautious. Or it *had*. It seemed like all her caution was gone when it came to Tristan.

The elevator doors opened, and she felt like she could breathe again. At least being in an open space with a lot of people milling around would keep them busy and away from each other. "We're here!" She squeaked and slipped around him. "Guess it's time to be all experiencey."

"Guess so." He stepped off the elevator with her and pulled out his phone. "Want to check out the bar? Get some juice?"

"Um, sure."

"I'm a little exhausted. Are you?" Tristan asked as they crossed the room to the bar.

Belle glanced at him, and she could tell he'd had a hard time sleeping the night before. "No, but are you okay?"

"I had a lot on my mind." He rubbed his eyes and tried to stifle a yawn.

Her desire to take care of him flared. "We'll make sure you get some rest tonight, okay?" Where had that come from? Ugh. Just. Met. Him. If she needed to, she'd get a permanent marker and write it on her hand.

His smile spread a warmth through her she'd never experienced with Paul. "Thanks."

"Sure." Man, she needed to get a grip.

After spending the day meandering around the ship, they made their way to the dining hall for dinner. They'd had lunch in one of the smaller restaurants. It had been okay, but Belle wasn't sure she could say that in her review at the end of the trip. They'd said she should be honest, but she didn't get that feeling at all from the lady when she first picked up her ticket.

Standing in the dinner buffet line, she lifted her head to glance around the room and couldn't believe her eyes. The color drained from her face, and her heart raced.

Laura and Paul. They were walking toward her. Why here? Why this ship? Why couldn't she make her feet work so she could run? They were glued to the floor. It felt like she couldn't breathe or think. The whole world was tilting sideways.

"Belle, are you okay?" Tristan's voice sounded a million miles away as the two people she never wanted to see again approached her.

She shook her head as they stopped in front of her.

"Oh, Belle, it's so good to see you!" Laura said. It suddenly dawned on Belle why Laura had been calling her so much the day before. She was going to be on this cruise. It made her wish she'd answered the phone call. She'd never have stepped foot on the boat.

Belle opened and shut her mouth as her gaze darted from Laura to Paul. "I, uh, uh…"

Tristan stuck his hand out. "I'm Tristan Davis. And you are?"

The woman smiled. "I'm Laura Denning, Belle's best friend, and this is Paul Whitlock, my fiancé."

"You are not my fr—Fiancé?" Belle finally found her voice, but it became a whisper as she realized what Laura had said.

Laura looked at Belle sympathetically. "I've been trying to call you, but you won't answer. I know things didn't go like I wanted, but you're still my best friend, even if you don't feel the same about me. I've missed you so much."

Just how crazy was she? "Things didn't go like you wanted? I'd say they went exactly how you wanted, based on the fact that you're engaged." Belle looked at Paul. "Fiancé?"

"That's typically what happens when you ask someone to marry you, Belle. Surely, you haven't forgotten that." The knife in her back felt like it'd just been twisted. Maybe she could fake a heart attack and get an emergency rescue.

"But…" She looked at Laura. "I…"

Paul looked down his long, crooked nose at her. "Are you taking a break before finding a new job?"

She didn't owe him any explanations. He was the reason she'd been driven out of marketing. Her cheeks burned, and her eyes narrowed. "I don't have to tell you anything since we're no longer engaged."

Laura punched Paul. "Stop that." She took Belle's hand. "Please, Belle, let's get a drink and the three of us can talk. Please?"

Pulling her hand away, Belle set her plate on the buffet and wrapped her arms around Tristan's bicep, shaking her head. "I don't have anything to talk about, and I'm not going to leave him just standing here. It would be rude." She didn't want to talk to Laura or Paul, and she certainly didn't want to talk to them together. Especially not here.

Paul narrowed his eyes as he looked at Tristan. "Don't I know you from somewhere?"

Belle looked at Tristan. He didn't look like anyone Paul would know.

Tristan shook his head. "No, I don't think so."

"You just look so familiar," Paul reiterated before returned his attention to Belle. "You were brilliant at marketing. I can't see you being unemployed long."

"Not brilliant enough," Belle mumbled. If she was so brilliant, she would've seen the double-cross coming. "Why are you here?"

Laura looked at her sheepishly. "I kinda booked it the moment I heard the radio announce you'd won."

Belle rolled her eyes. Of course that's what happened. Her former best friend had been desperate to make amends, despite Belle's resistance. Why did she have to ruin her vacation? Couldn't she take the hint? Why did she think it was okay to just show up?

She grabbed Belle's hand again. "Come on; I'll use our room card, and it'll be on me. And I won't take no for an answer. We're stuck on this ship for eight more days, so we might as well talk now." Laura looked at Tristan. "You can come too."

Belle jerked her hand away, and Tristan stepped between them. "She doesn't seem all that thrilled to see you. I think you need to leave her alone."

Laura turned her face up to him. "She's my best friend. I made a huge mistake."

"And sometimes, mistakes can't be fixed. She's obviously upset."

Belle touched his shoulder, appreciating his protectiveness. He was right, sometimes a mistake couldn't be fixed, but he didn't understand. Laura was like this because of Belle letting her walk all over her in the past. This was her chance to set Laura straight. "I don't want to talk, Laura. Why can't you understand?"

"I do understand. I swear. I just want a chance to show you how sorry I am. I love you, and I miss you. I did a horrible thing. Please, please, just give me a minute."

In her mind, she wanted to scream. Laura would follow her around the entire cruise. It's what Laura did. She'd keep bugging her until she got what she wanted. Everything was about her. All Belle wanted was to enjoy the cruise. She didn't want to deal with Laura or Paul or the drama that seemed to follow them.

As much as she didn't want to talk to Laura, she wanted even more to be left alone. If suffering through a few minutes of talking got them to leave her alone, it was worth it, even if it meant Laura getting what she wanted. She'd stand firm this time though. Their friendship was over. Dead and buried.

"Fine, but we aren't friends. And we are definitely not spending this cruise together." Belle loosened her grip on Tristan's bicep but stayed close to him as she followed Laura and Paul into the bar. The couple led them to an area that seemed a little off to the side and out of the way. Two love seats sat across from each other with a narrow table separating them.

"Paul, darling, would you get us some drinks. You

know what I like." She looked at Tristan and then Belle. "How about you two?"

Darling? Her stomach twisted. There were so many things wrong with her and Laura's relationship. Why hadn't she seen it before? What was wrong with her that she couldn't break away from her? A little voice whispered, "Because she's all you've had for so long, and living without her has been hard." It was a toxic relationship, and she knew that. But it wasn't as simple as walking away.

"I'll have water," said Tristan.

Belle nodded. "Same."

Laura looked deflated. "Oh, come on."

"I don't drink." Tristan looked at Belle. "If you want something, go ahead."

"No, I think I'll stick with water." She smiled. What did she care if Laura was sad? It was her fault their friendship had ended.

Laura shrugged. "Okay, water it is."

Paul glanced at the three of them and left.

"So, how have you been? It's been months since we talked. How's your mom? I tried calling, but the nursing home said she'd moved." Laura sat on the edge of her seat with her hands in her lap.

Belle swallowed hard. She didn't want to talk about her mom. Not in front of Tristan. Not yet, anyway. It wasn't the right time. "Uh, I don't think it's a good idea to get too personal."

"What? We're best friends." Laura stood and moved to sit on the coffee table in front of Belle. "I know I hurt you. I should have handled it better. Been more honest. I just didn't know how. I'm so sorry."

"We are not friends, Laura. You broke my heart. This isn't something you say sorry for and it's suddenly better." Belle looked down and, gritting her teeth, she said, "You were dating my fiancé behind my back. You believed everything he said about me. We've known each other since high school, and yet his word was worth more than mine."

"I know, and I'm sorry. But you have to admit, you did seem a little crazy." Laura twisted her fingers in the hem of her shirt. "It was hard to dismiss what he was saying."

Belle exhaled sharply. "You should have because you and I were friends, but you believed him." Laura deserved Paul. No, they deserved each other.

Paul returned and set the drinks on the table. "What did I miss?"

Laura bounced up and took her seat next to Paul. "Nothing." She took a sip of a tall fruity-looking drink. "So, Tristan, have you known Belle long?"

"We've been dating four months." It flew out of her

mouth like a gust of wind. She said it without even thinking. They thought she was pathetic, but she didn't have to be single. She looked at Tristan, not sure if she wanted him to play along or not. If he did, she was sure he'd have questions later. What kind of mess was she getting herself into? Maybe she should just stop it before it got started. No, once this little meeting was over, her pretend relationship would be too.

Tristan put his arm across her shoulders. "And it's been a great four months. Isn't that right, love?"

"Perfect." Belle was so relieved she almost kissed him. Talk about a disaster.

Paul leaned back in his seat and slipped his arm around Laura's waist. "Four months? I guess you can't be too mad at us, then, seeing that we broke up only six months ago."

"I guess you couldn't have been too in love with me, seeing as you're already engaged to Laura, not to mention cheating on me with her while we were engaged." There was no way she was going to use the words best friend where Laura was concerned. What a joke. Friends didn't do what Laura did.

"You went off the deep end. I didn't plan on falling in love with Laura; it just happened. We were worried about you, and over time, we developed feelings for each other." The smile he gave her was almost imperceptible. He was such a snake. He didn't love Laura either. More than likely, he was using her too. She didn't care this time. Laura had gone out with guys in the past, and Belle had come to her rescue. Not this time. She was on her own.

Tristan pulled Belle closer to him. "Then I should thank you. Belle is something special, and I would have hated missing out on being with her."

Her skin broke out in goosebumps. Boy, he was convincing. If she didn't know any better, she'd even believe him. Belle covered his hand with hers. "Being mad about you two...dating," the word felt bitter in her mouth, "would *not* keep me from moving on."

She wouldn't go into the other part of it. The part where Paul had started doing things that made her look bad. Things like changing her appointments in her calendar so she was late, changing clients' names so she called them by the wrong name, or rescheduling dinner reservations and then telling people she was making it all up.

"Does that mean we can try to be friends again?" Laura asked. "I've missed you terribly."

Belle stiffened. She hated that Paul had come between them, but she wasn't sure she could forgive Laura for taking his side and having an affair with him. Even if she could forgive her, she'd never trust her again. That was a wound that wouldn't ever be completely healed. After all they'd been through, it was his word against hers. "No. You hurt me. I could never trust you again." She hadn't meant to just say it, but there it was. It was how she felt, and it was out now.

"I know, and I will do everything I can to make it up to you." Laura smiled. "I know. You and Tristan can join us for a show and dinner tomorrow night."

"We're busy," Belle said a little too eagerly. "Sorry."

Laura looked at Paul and then back to Belle. "Busy with what?"

"We'd planned on relaxing on the deck," Tristan said. "So, sorry, the answer's no. I don't really want to share her anyway."

A thrill shot through Belle. She barely knew Tristan, and he was already treating her better than anyone ever had. She looked at him, and her mouth went dry. He was looking at her like he meant every word. "Yeah, sorry, no," she said as she kept her eyes on him.

Laura's lips curved into a wide, toothy smile. "Please. I'm begging you. Just have dinner with us. We both want you to have dinner with us, right, honey?"

"Anything you want, darling." Paul took her chin in his fingers and kissed her.

Belle's stomach twisted again. She wished she could throw up on his shoes.

"Like I said, we've got plans, so we'll have to decline the dinner invite." Belle tugged on Tristan's hand. "Okay, well, we'd better get going. Winning the trip came with stipulations. We need to explore."

Tristan stood with her and laced his fingers in hers. "We'll see you around, I guess."

Laura quickly stood. "Please, Belle. Please. I'll do anything if you'll have dinner with us."

Anything, huh? Like leave her alone for the rest of the cruise? Was it worth it to be free of her? She was so tired of being pushed around by Laura. At least this way, she could get something out of it. Hopefully. Laura had a habit of making deals and then breaking them. "Fine, but you have to leave me alone the rest of the cruise. That means I'm off limits. Got it?"

Laura pouted. "I guess."

"I mean it, Laura."

"Okay, yes. I'll leave you alone if you have dinner with us." She bit her lip. "There's a five-star restaurant up top, and it'll be chef's choice. It's supposed to be super fancy and wonderful."

Ugh. Why couldn't Laura just...stop being so

Laura? "Okay, then. We'll have dinner with you. But that's it. You leave me alone the rest of the cruise."

"Okay, we'll meet you tomorrow at seven." Laura gave her a little smile and wiggled her fingers in a goodbye.

Belle pulled Tristan through the bar, and the last thing she saw before the crowd blocked her view was Paul and Laura smooching.

Outside, Belle lifted up on her tiptoes and put her lips to Tristan's ear. She needed time to figure out what she could say about roping Tristan into being her boyfriend. Something other than she was just plain pathetic. "Can we talk about what happened in there a little later?" She paused. "But thank you for playing along. I'm sorry."

Tristan tucked a piece of her hair behind her ear. "He's a jerk, and you deserve better."

He was so sweet for helping her out. When she'd blurted it out, she didn't expect she'd have to continue the charade. Why couldn't Laura just take the hint that their friendship was over? It wasn't even a hint. Belle had outright said she was done with her. With both of them. That was Laura though. There were rocks that weren't as dense.

Why did things have to be so complicated? She'd gone on a cruise to get away from everything, and now everything she wanted to get away from was confined to a boat she couldn't escape. Maybe if she jumped overboard, the Coast Guard or Navy could rescue her. No, she might be crazy, but she wasn't nuts.

CHAPTER 5

A knock came on Tristan's door, and he quickly opened it. "Hey."

"Hi," Belle said and hesitated at the door. "I'm really sorry for telling them we're dating. I'll just 'fess up so you don't have to deal with it." Her hair was damp, and she had on flannel pajama pants with big red conversation hearts and a light-pink shirt that matched. She was downright adorable.

Tristan took her elbow and gently pulled her in. Her coconut scent filled the room the moment he closed the door behind her. "It's okay, but we probably need to learn a little more about each other before we have dinner with them tomorrow night."

He'd looked forward to getting to know her all night. The only thing that worried him even slightly

was that Paul acted suspicious, and he remembered
Belle telling him that Laura kept up with society
gossip.

"Are you sure? I don't want you to feel like I'm
using you." Her bottom lip was captured between her
teeth, and the look she was giving him made it hard to
breathe.

He didn't feel used at all. "Yeah, I'm sure." And he
didn't want her stuck with Laura without someone
around to step in if she needed it.

When she blurted out they were dating, he'd gone
with it because, in truth, he liked the idea of dating
her. She was sweet, kind, and caring—qualities he
wanted in a woman he dated or possibly fell for.
What? Good grief, he needed to get a handle on things.
He was there to observe the crew and blend in, not get
googly-eyed over a woman.

She looked around the room. "Huh, our beds share
the same wall. I even have the same upholstered chair
in my room." Belle sat down in the chair and fidgeted
with her fingers. "I'm so sorry."

"Stop. If I had minded, I wouldn't have played
along." He took a seat on the edge of the bed across
from her.

Belle smiled. "I hadn't thought about it like that,
but that's true."

"When's your birthday?" he asked.

"It's the last day of this cruise, June fifth. I'll be thirty."

Tristan nodded. "September twenty-nine, and I'll be thirty-two. I'm surprised you're so open with your age."

She shrugged and seemed to relax. "I don't want to look older than I am, but I don't care about aging."

"Laura said something about your mom." Tristan was most curious about it. Belle had dodged the question deftly.

Belle chewed her thumb and stood. A quiet sigh left her lips, and she looked at him. "My mom hasn't been well."

"I'm sorry." Tristan balanced his elbows on his thighs. "That has to be hard."

"It is, but she's getting great care. That's what matters." She turned and a weak smile played on her lips. There was more to the story, but she needed to be ready to tell him.

He nodded. "You're right; that's all that matters."

"What should I know about you?" she asked as she took her seat again.

That was a loaded question, but he settled on telling her about his parents. No one really knew much about that. "My parents were killed in a plane crash when I was ten. They were coming back from a business meeting, and it went down during a freak rainstorm. By the time the plane was found, they were both gone."

"Oh, Tristan," she said, leaning forward. Her fingers curved around his wrist, and she looked at him. "I… That's awful. I'm so sorry that happened to you. Who took care of you after that?"

"My grandma." Inwardly, he smacked himself. It had just come out. Everything was so easy with Belle. How was he so comfortable with her already?

She slipped out of the chair and onto the floor in front of him. "I bet she loved you to pieces. I bet she was wonderful and sweet, just like you." She slapped a hand over her mouth. "I'm sorry."

"You're sorry for complimenting me?" He chuckled.

Her eyes held his a second longer before she looked down. "No, I just…I don't know you very well, and I don't want things to be weird. I like having a friend." She looked up, and her eyes were so dark-green they almost looked black. "I've been so lonely, and it's nice having someone to talk to."

Boy, was the feeling mutual. "I feel the same way."

"You look tired. Maybe we can continue this tomorrow?"

Now that she said it, he wasn't tired; he was exhausted. He tried to hold back the yawn and failed. "I am. I'm sorry."

"Do you think you can sleep?" He could see the concern in her eyes.

No. "It'd be a lie if I said yes. It's usually worse when I'm this tired. It's like my mind starts down this spiral, and I can't stop it."

"Would it make things awkward if I tried something?" She held her bottom lip with her teeth, and her eyebrows knitted together.

At this point? He didn't care if it did. "I'm so tired I'm willing to risk it."

"Okay, lie down."

He did as she asked, and she sat beside him. Bracing one hand on the bed, she leaned over him. "My mom did this to me when I was a kid. I don't know why, but it always knocked me out."

If it worked, he was all for it. "I'll take it."

"Don't take this the wrong way. It's just to help you sleep." She gave him a pointed look.

He shook his head. "I won't." What could she possibly do that would give him the wrong impression? The question was barely a thought, when cool fingers slid through his hair, right at his temple. It was so simple and innocent, and at the same time, it was the most intimate thing he'd ever experienced. His body relaxed like it was a command as she continued to comb her fingers through his hair. His eyelids grew heavy and slid shut.

"That feels really good."

"Good." Her voice was just as soothing as her fingers running through his hair.

He nodded, but her words were muffled. A few deep breaths, and he felt himself drifting.

"Goodnight," she said.

He could have sworn she kissed his forehead. That couldn't be, though; they were friends. He was really tired too, so he'd probably only imagined it. The last thing he heard was the click of a door.

BELLE WAITED for Tristan at the entrance to the dining room. Her day had started earlier than she wanted, but she'd woken up full of energy. She'd also woken up with Tristan on her mind. What was she thinking, kissing him on the forehead? Her only saving grace was that he was sound asleep.

As she'd stroked his hair, his body relaxed, and he looked so peaceful. Moments later, he was breathing evenly. It took every ounce of restraint she had not to run her fingertips over his lips and cheeks.

It had taken her a while to fall asleep too. She'd remembered counting to at least five hundred and something. She could not fall for Tristan. He was her friend, and that's what she needed. *Only* a friend. Her brain balked as she thought about setting it on repeat.

She discreetly pulled out her phone and looked at the time. It was almost ten in the morning. He had less than five minutes and he'd miss breakfast. Had he set an alarm? Oh gosh, maybe he hadn't. Maybe he thought she would do it before she left.

Just as she began to panic, Tristan appeared across the way, and butterflies tickled her stomach.

"Stop that," she murmured and rubbed her midsection. He was just a guy. A really nice, sexy guy who made her all squishy. Ugh. If she could, she'd throw herself down on the floor and throw a full-on tantrum.

His lips spread into a smile that went to his eyes. Not the flirty one, but this one was growing on her.

"Hey," he said as he stopped in front of her. He'd worn a solid light-gray button-up shirt and dark-gray slacks, and he always smelled like spice. Today, she caught a hint of aftershave with it, and it only made it better.

Belle lifted up on her toes and realized she was halfway through an actual bounce. She was bouncing. Taking a deep breath, she set herself back on the floor and hoped he didn't see it. What was her issue? She was frustrated with herself. Straightening her shoulders, she renewed her resolution to just be friends. "Hi. Do you feel better this morning?"

Tristan shot her that sexy half-smile with the exclamation point dimple. "I do."

Without her permission, her lips curved into a smile in response. "I told you it worked." Yeah, she was flirting. She shouldn't have been, but it was harmless as long as there was no touching involved.

Then his hand grazed her elbow and left a trail of goosebumps as it slid down her arm. She bit the inside of her cheek to keep from yelping.

"And you were right. Thank you. For staying and helping me." His eyes held hers, and there was such a depth of sincerity she could almost drown in them.

Before she could stop herself, she lifted on her tiptoes and brushed his cheek with the back of her hand. "You're so sweet. Who wouldn't want to stay and help you?" What? What did she just do? Why did she say that? Geez. She needed to get herself under control.

"I don't have very many people in my life who care.

At least, not about me as a person. Mostly people like to use me." Tristan stiffened as a look of sadness crossed his face and stepped back. "We're still on for tonight, right?"

Belle's heart dropped to the floor. *She'd* used him. "Tristan, I am so sorry for roping you into this pretend-dating thing."

He held his hand up and smiled. "Of all the things I've been used for, this is the best so far." He winked. "I really don't mind."

Belle's head bobbled like a doll. Oh, for heaven's sake, what was it about Tristan Davis that made her head so dizzy she couldn't speak and her knees so weak she needed something to hold on to?

She followed him to the buffet, and they slowly filled their plates. From time to time, she glanced over at him, just to make sure he was really okay. People had used him, and she didn't want to be one of those people, even if he had said he didn't mind.

Concentrating on breakfast kept her mind off of him for a second. She needed to stop being so twitter-pated when it came to him. He was just a guy. A really, really hot guy who was sweet...candy sweet.

What kind of lousy pep talk was that? She smacked her forehead and realized she'd actually done it. There was no way to make that spastic move smooth, so she lowered her hand, feeling grateful Tristan had been looking down when she did it. Not only was it the worst pep talk in history, but people in the dining room had to be wondering if she was losing her mind.

People? She was wondering herself. A small giggle popped out, and she covered her mouth with her hand, glancing up to see if he'd heard her. Luckily, when she peeked at Tristan, he was busy talking to a few passengers ahead of him in line.

Inwardly, she groaned. If she was this nuts at dinner, Paul was going to be rolling in the aisle, laughing at her. She could only imagine what Laura would think. Why had she agreed to have dinner with them?

It *was* a cruise ship. Would it be wrong to pray for a ship-wide, unknown virus to break out? Yeah, it was, but at least she wouldn't have to have dinner with Paul and Laura.

With nine hours to dwell on it, she was sure she'd be certifiably insane by the time dinner rolled around.

CHAPTER 6

Tristan double-checked his cufflinks and slipped on his suit coat. It was a good thing he'd gone with his gut and brought one. Checking himself in the mirror one last time, he straightened his black necktie and headed out the door. His imagination had gone wild all day. He knew Belle would look great, and he couldn't wait to see her.

Excitement made his stomach dip and dive. He wasn't sure why he was so nervous. It wasn't like he hadn't been to dinner with a beautiful woman before. Still, dinner with Belle, even if he did have to share her, was exhilarating.

He took a gulp of air and tried to calm his anxiety. It was a fake date, and he needed to remember that. She'd made it clear she didn't want to be in a relationship. Belle saw him as a friend, and he needed to respect that. He wanted a friend too. He didn't know her well enough yet, and he wasn't necessarily looking for a relationship either.

Another deep breath, and he tapped on the door.

"Just a second." Her voice carried through it.

He jammed his hands in his pockets and smiled at a passenger as they went into their room across the hall. The door opened, and his breath caught. His brain caught up, and he said, "Wow."

"Is it okay?" She ran her palm down the side of the dress and then looked up at him.

Okay? She was stunning. The dark-blue off-the-shoulder floor-length dress made her skin look so soft he wanted to touch her, and her curled hair bounced around her shoulders. "Jewels look dull in comparison. You're breathtaking."

A dark-pink blush covered her cheeks and only added to her beauty. "Thank you. I'm kinda nervous." She pulled the little cover over her arms a little tighter.

"You have no reason to be." That was an understatement. He held out his arm, and she hooked hers through it.

She glanced at him. "You look incredible, like you stepped out of a magazine."

"We must have been on the same page, then." He winked as they stopped at the elevator.

The rosy color returned, and she pressed her hand to her cheek. "I'm going to get a big head if you don't stop."

"I'm sorry, but I have to call 'em like I see 'em." The elevator doors opened, and they stepped inside. What was he doing? He had to stop flirting. He was acting like he needed behavior reconditioning. Maybe that's what he'd do. He'd get a rubber band for his wrist and snap it every time he did something stupid.

As soon as the doors shut, she turned to him. "Could you bend down a little?"

He did as she asked, thinking his tie was probably crooked.

"Close your eyes," she whispered.

Tristan closed his eyes. "Is something on my face?" That would be truly embarrassing, but at least she was catching it before they got to dinner.

"No," she said, and her soft lips lightly caressed his.

His eyes popped open, and his lips parted in shock. She'd kissed him. He was going to need another rubber band, maybe even dozens.

"We're dating. It occurred to me that we might not want to look like we're shocked if we need to kiss later. Paul is pretty good at spotting fakes, and…" She shrugged one shoulder.

Tristan darted his gaze to the floor number above the elevator door. They had ten more floors.

She gasped as he pulled her to him and stared into her eyes. "Maybe we should make sure it looks like we've kissed more than once?"

"Okay." The word was nearly inaudible.

His lips met hers, and a groan came from deep in his throat. It'd been too long since he'd kissed someone he was more than casually interested in. She caressed his cheek with the back of her hand and then laced her fingers in his hair. The sensation sent a thrill all the way down his spine.

Tristan broke the kiss long enough to pick her up by the waist and press her against the elevator wall. Seven floors left, and all he could think was that it wasn't enough time.

Belle held his gaze for a heartbeat, and then her lips brushed his like feathers, teasing and taunting him. He felt like he'd been hit with vertigo. His head swam, his ears rang, and if his heart beat any faster, he'd need medical attention.

When he could take it no longer, he sank his fingers into her hair and deepened the kiss. He'd kissed women he was attracted to before, but this was a wholly different and unique experience. This was deeper than attraction. Belle made him feel things he hadn't felt before with anyone. Her body conformed to his, and they continued to kiss as he felt the elevator slowing to a stop. Why did she have to kiss him in the elevator? He wasn't ready to stop kissing her.

With no choice, he pulled back just as the elevator dinged, and he set her down as the doors opened. His lungs burned as he tried to get enough air. When he noticed Belle looked as flushed he felt, a jolt went through him. Was there a possibility she felt the same thing he did?

She palmed her chest, and he followed her out. Then she turned and tiptoed. "We probably need to keep that to a minimum if we don't want things to get confusing."

Confusing? How about mind-blowing? If that was a fake-date kiss, what would a real kiss be like? Suddenly, he was aching to find out.

He balled his hands into fists and mentally chastised himself. A little kiss from her, and he was losing it. It had to stop. He had to stop.

She rubbed her thumb across his lips. "That lipstick stain isn't your color." She held her bottom lip in her teeth as she tried not to smile, and her eyes glinted mischievously.

Tristan chuckled. "Probably not." He took her hand and put it around his arm. As they walked, all he could think was that he wished he didn't have to share her. Sitting through dinner with Paul and Laura was going to be torture.

When they reached the dining room, Laura was waiting for them at the entrance. "I almost thought you weren't coming."

Belle gave him a small smile, and her eyes sparkled. "Sorry. We had…something come up."

"I had them sit us away from the crowd. That way we can hear each other." Laura tried to slip her arm in Belle's, but she quickly avoided it by hooking her hand around Tristan's bicep. He smiled and enjoyed how her body felt next to his.

Laura frowned but didn't say anything.

Paul stood when they reached the table. "Nice to see you two again."

"I told him he had to behave tonight, or else." Laura took her place next to him.

"Good luck with that," Belle said under her breath as Tristan held the seat for her.

Laura clapped her hands together. "I'm so excited." She stretched her hands across the table and took Belle's hands in hers. Belle stiffened. "I've missed you. I have so much to tell you."

"Okay. Tell away." Belle's eyes were trained on the hands holding hers, and her voice sounded strained. Tristan couldn't believe Laura was so insistent on touching Belle when she obviously didn't want to be touched.

He pulled Belle's hands from Laura's. "I'm sharing enough as it is. I think I'll hold her hands," he said.

Belle gave him a smile and squeezed his hands before letting go, like it was a silent thank you.

"You're engaged, right?" Belle asked.

"Yes, and," she looked at Paul, "we're getting married when we dock in St. Thomas."

BELLE JERKED HER HEAD UP. "That's...fast."

"I know, but we're so in love." Laura snuggled into Paul.

Paul kissed Laura on the cheek. "I figured it was perfect timing."

"Right." She looked from Paul to Laura. Belle didn't know what to do. Laura thought she knew Paul, but she didn't. "Isn't that a little too fast? Didn't you always say you wanted a huge wedding?"

Laura shrugged. "I know, but it isn't about the big wedding. It's about two people who love each other.

Anyway, I know it might be a little awkward, but..."
She paused.

Belle's stomach dropped to the floor. No, she wouldn't. Not after what happened. Surely, the girl had more common sense than that. But it *was* Laura. Common sense was not one of her attributes.

"I'd like you to be my maid of honor." Laura beamed.

The words had spilled out, and Belle felt ill. How could she ask her to do this? Like they were fast friends. They weren't. She hung her head, trying to settle her thoughts and calm her racing heart. "Why?" she asked and looked up.

Her friend, or ex-friend—oh, she didn't know what to call her—shrugged. "You're my best friend. It wouldn't be the same without you there."

Belle was speechless. No, flabbergasted. How could Laura ask that of her? And why was she even sitting there listening? After what Laura did? It wasn't that Paul cheated on Belle. Yes, that hurt, but Laura had broken her heart. She looked at Tristan. "I..."

Tristan wrapped his arm around her shoulders and looked at Laura. "Maybe give her some time to digest it, okay? But if she says no, then the answer is no. I won't let you hurt her again."

"Sure."

He'd rescued her. It might have seemed insignificant to anyone on the outside looking in, but she'd never be able to thank him enough. Under the table, she covered his hand with hers and squeezed, and then she put her lips to his ear. "Thank you."

When she pulled back, his eyes held hers. "Anytime."

A waiter stopped at the table just as she leaned in to kiss him. "What can I get you guys to drink?"

It was probably a good thing. Kissing him would have definitely made things confusing. More than they already were. That kiss in the elevator was toe-curling amazing. One thing Tristan had down was how to kiss. Just thinking about it made her head swim and goosebumps cover her body.

They gave the waiter their drink orders, and he left, taking the heaviness that had been in the air with him.

"So, are you guys going to explore Grand Turk?" asked Paul, directing the question to Belle.

Tristan scooted closer. "We'd planned on it." His fingers grazed her bare shoulder, and she shivered. He looked at her. "Are you cold?"

"Uh, no. I think it was just a current of air or something." Something named Tristan. Surprisingly, she wasn't cold at the moment. The little shawl she'd worn was doing its job.

He leaned down. "If you get cold, let me know. You can use my jacket."

She wished she could say thanks, but her tongue was so tied she was sure it was in a bow. The four of them sat in silence until it became stifling uncomfortable.

"How did the two of you meet?" Laura asked.

Tristan gave her a half-smile. "We met on this ship, actually."

Laura tilted her head. "You've cruised on this ship before?"

Before Belle could answer or, well, think of a convincing lie, the waiter returned and served their drinks. "Dinner will be out in a few more minutes."

"But we didn't order," Belle said.

Laura reached across the table like she was going to touch Belle again, but Belle pulled her hand back. "You don't order here. It a four-course meal prepared by the chef. It's his choice."

"Oh, right. I forgot." Belle took a sip of her water. Why didn't she remember that?

Paul leveled his cold blue eyes at her. "She's probably used to eating cheap drive-thru."

Laura glared at him. "You promised you'd behave."

Paul shrugged. "I am. I'm teasing her."

"Well, stop it." She crossed her arms over her chest.

"Okay, okay. I'm sorry." He pulled her to him. "Forgive me?" Those same cold blue eyes looked at Laura like a drowning cat.

How was she going to survive this all night? How was she going to continue the fake relationship with Tristan? Maybe she should come clean. It's not like she cared what Paul thought anyway.

She just had to get through the next few days of being stuck on a boat with them, and then Laura and Paul would be gone and out of her life. Why didn't that make her happy? Wasn't that what she wanted? Everything was so confusing. Maybe after dinner, when the ship was quiet, she'd take a walk and try to clear her head.

For now, she'd smile and pretend she was okay. She could do that. Easy peasy.

CHAPTER 7

Tristan sat up the second he heard Belle's door open and shut. Dinner had been a mixture of wonderful and awful. Wonderful because he was with her, and awful because she looked so uncomfortable.

She'd been there for him, and he wanted to be there for her. Friends were there for each other, right? He didn't even bother putting on shoes before running out the door to catch up with her.

"Hey, are you okay?"

"Yeah, I'm fine." She wouldn't look at him, and her voice trembled.

"You don't sound fine." He took her by the arms and made her face him. "How can I help?"

Tear-filled eyes peered up at him. "Want to take a walk? I wore my best pajamas."

He chuckled and waved a hand down his body. "So did I. These are all the rage in Paris."

Belle choked out a laugh. "I can tell. You look dashing."

"Where do you want to walk?" He'd follow her anywhere she wanted to go.

She lifted a shaky hand to her lips, and she swallowed hard. "I thought fresh air would be good."

Tristan pushed the up button to the elevator, and they got on when the doors popped open. "We'll be in Grand Turk in a few hours. Are you going to do a little sightseeing?" If she was, he was going with her.

She leaned her back against the elevator wall. "I don't know. Maybe. Laura will be bugging me to hang out with her, despite her promise not to. That's Laura though. She's always been like that."

Visions of pressing her against the wall flooded him, and he pushed them down. She was hurting. She didn't need him thinking like that. He didn't need him thinking like that. It was a fake kiss. "You can say no." He was still trying to comprehend how someone like Belle was friends with someone like Laura.

A nod of her head, and she was quiet the rest of the way up. He understood betrayal. It was soul-crushing when someone you trusted turned out to be someone who wanted to use you. He knew that feeling all too well.

The elevator doors opened, and they continued in silence until they got to the railing. Her head fell back, and she took deep breaths, letting them out slowly. "Someone told me that salt air was good for cleansing. Wise woman, but I think I'll need to do it a few hundred more times."

His grandmother would have loved her, and the thought made him smile. "Yeah, I think it took more than once."

She crossed her arms on the railing and leaned forward. "She wants me to be the maid of honor at her wedding."

He knew that was what was bothering her. "What are you going to do?"

"I have no idea. I have two days to mull it over, and in the meantime, I can hear her asking me about it like a kid asking her parents, 'Are we there yet?'" She shivered and hugged herself. "I don't know why I'm even considering it. I feel broken or something."

Instinct took over, and Tristan put his arms around her. "If you're cold, we can go back inside."

"I don't want to." She snuggled into him. It took a strength he didn't know he had not to tip her chin up and kiss her. He needed to remember his rubber band next time.

"What do you want to do? I guess that's a better question." A brisk wind hit his feet, and he realized they were freezing. He had Belle in his arms, though, and he wasn't about to move.

She leaned back and looked up at him. "I want to toss them both overboard."

Tristan threw his head back and laughed. "Prison wouldn't be a good look for you."

"Yeah, I know. Seeing them again just dredged up all these feelings I thought I'd dealt with, but I guess I hadn't. Not so much him, but Laura. I want to hate her because of how much she hurt me, but at the same time, I don't want to hold onto all this anger. I want to be friends with her because I miss her. I know I shouldn't, but I do. What's wrong with me?"

He hated that she was hurting so much. "Nothing's wrong with you. Feelings are never as straightforward as we need them to be."

"No, and I'm not even upset about their dating. I don't even care now. Well, I care because he's a snake and she doesn't see it. If I try to warn her, though, she'll just think I made it up."

She drew circles on his t-shirt with her fingers. It

was messing with his head. Not that she was doing it deliberately, but it was.

"If I asked what happened, would you tell me?" He hoped she'd trust him enough to tell him.

She touched his arms, and her eyes locked with his. "You're freezing."

"I'm good."

"Hold that thought." She dashed away and returned a few minutes later with a large blanket.

Tristan eyed her. "Did you go all the way to your room to get that?"

"No way. In that brochure they gave us, it said they stashed them around the ship. I just had to find one."

The smile she gave him made his pulse jump. He'd known her all of three days, but there was something drawing him to her.

"Lay down on that lounge, and I'll cover us up."

When he got settled, she flung a blanket over his legs then covered them both with another one. "I didn't realize you got two blankets."

She shrugged. "You're out here in bare feet. I bet they're freezing. No point in making you suffer because I'm short. Plus, I'm always cold. It can be eighty, and I've got a sweater on."

He usually ran cold too. Now that he thought

about it, she'd been wearing sweaters every time he'd seen her.

"Do you always do this?" he asked as she lay down facing him.

Her eyebrows knitted together. "Do what?"

"Take care of people like this?"

For more heartbeats than he liked, she paused, and then she looked him in the eyes. It looked like she was trying to find the right words. "To a degree, yes. I can't stand to see anyone hurting. Not people. Not animals. I just can't do it."

Her answer didn't surprise him at all, but he wasn't sure she'd given him the full answer. He wouldn't press her about it. He was more interested in her history with Paul. "Back to your story. Will you tell me what happened?"

BELLE HAD KNOWN he'd ask sooner or later, and he deserved an answer. He'd rescued her by playing along as her fake boyfriend, and then he'd rescued her again during dinner when she was stunned speechless.

"It took me a while to figure out what I wanted to be when I grew up, so I was a little older when I graduated." He didn't need to know part of the reason it took so long was she was taking care of her mom.

"How old were you when you graduated?"

"Twenty-six. I knew marketing was it the moment I opened the first textbook. I loved being creative and coming up with unique ideas." She could hear the happiness in her own voice. Until this moment, it hadn't hit her how much she missed her old job.

Tristan pulled the covers up as the wind blew harder. They were now almost completely under the blanket. "That wind has a bite to it."

She inched herself closer to him. "Yeah, tonight it does. I bet there's a storm somewhere out there."

"Okay, you love marketing. What happened to make you quit?" His arm draped across her waist, and the palm of his hand was flat on her back. He made it almost impossible to keep her mind on the story.

This was it. She'd never told anyone what had happened. The next day, she'd handed in her resignation, packed her apartment up, and left Dallas with her mom. It had worked out well for her mom. The nursing home in Miami was so much better than anywhere else she'd found.

"Long story short, I was working for the Epstein Marketing Group in Dallas. Paul and I were on a team, and it got competitive. I ended up resigning."

"Could I get the version that's a little longer?"

The long version still stung. "We were put on a team together, and we clicked. It wasn't long before we started dating. Anyway, our campaigns got noticed, we moved up, and the agency was looking to reel in this company out of Dallas." Belle covered her mouth as she yawned. "Sorry."

Tristan yawned as well. "That's contagious, but go ahead."

"Paul and I were told that one of us would be in charge of that account. We were basically competing against each other. I didn't understand it because we had made a name for ourselves working together, but I approached it like I did everything. I was going to give my best, and if that was enough, great. If not, then I would congratulate Paul. Only he didn't see it that way." While she'd talked, Tristan had rolled onto his back, and she found herself cuddled under his arm with her head on his shoulder. She should move. Put distance between them. But after months of being on her own, it was nice to have a friend. Someone she felt comfortable with.

"He got competitive?"

"More than that. They gave us six weeks to present our idea. The campaign they picked would determine the winner. The first couple of meetings we had with the company, we were just supposed to be getting an idea of what they wanted. I know I entered the correct date and time in my planner, but the time had been changed. When I got to the office, the meeting was over, and they were all leaving. I looked like a flake because I'd arrived late."

"What else?"

"Names were changed in my planner. All sorts of little things, but I sounded completely paranoid because when I'd go to show it to someone, it'd be changed back. Laura was my roommate at the time, and, of course, she knew Paul from the very beginning. Once the competition started, everything happened so fast. Paul convinced her the stress was getting to me. He made it sound like I was losing my mind. Three weeks before the presentation, Paul dumped me for Laura, and I found out he had been cheating on me with her. At that point, it felt like the world was just crashing in around me. When it came time for the presentation, I was a basket case because I was so afraid of missing it. I completely blew it. I resigned the next day." Belle stretched her arm across Tristan's chest and propped her head in her hand.

"That's awful."

"Yeah, I was humiliated. I looked and sounded deranged. I hadn't slept or eaten. I'd never felt so out of control in my life. But it was all me. That is, until I took my tablet to a computer repair store. Paul didn't realize he was leaving a trail on it. I'd taken it in because the screen was blinking and some of my settings were messed up. When I went to pick it up, the guy working on it asked me about the access I had on it."

Tristan tiled his head. "Access?"

"Remote access. Somehow Paul had gotten into it, and I know it was him because the IP address led back to him. I also found out he'd done it before. It was why he left his last agency. He was forced out."

"Did you tell anyone after that?"

She laid her head back on his shoulder. "No, I was done. Even with that, there was no getting my crazy antics out of their heads. I behaved totally unprofessional. I should have taken it in the first time it happened."

"How were you to know?" He snagged a piece of her flyaway hair and tucked it behind her ear, and she realized how close they were.

Her body was pressed against his side, and her leg was over his. It was like they were a real couple. Her cheeks burned with embarrassment. When she tried to move, he stopped her.

"I'm comfortable," he said and shot her a half-smile, dimple included.

"I just don't want things to get confusing. I like having you as a friend. The last person I fell for put me through a cheese grater. I'm over him, but I'm not sure I'm ready for something new." It was better to be upfront. She didn't want to hurt him in case he mistook her.

Tristan wrapped his arms around her. "We're supposed to be dating."

That was true. Her mistake was looking up and locking eyes with him. She wasn't ready for something new, or she didn't think she was. "I just don't want to hurt you."

"How about this: if I think I'm on the verge of a broken heart, I'll let you know. In the meantime, we pretend to date. Maybe if Laura sees you've really moved on, she'll be more receptive to hearing your concerns about Paul."

"You do have a point."

"I know." He brushed his lips across her cheek, and she couldn't stop herself from leaning into him.

Oh man, she was doomed. Doomed, doomed, doomed. She threaded her fingers through his hair, and his lips hovered millimeters from hers. "That wasn't fair."

"I know."

"Um, excuse me?" A voice broke through the moment.

Belle pulled the blanket down and squeezed her eyes shut. Of course it'd be Laura.

"Belle?"

"Yeah."

Laura scrunched her face up. "I'm so, so sorry. I didn't realize it was you. I'm lost."

Tristan quietly groaned, and she couldn't say she didn't feel the same way.

"We were just getting ready to go anyway."

He shot her a look, and she grinned. They didn't need to be kissing. She was already confused and emotional. Saved by the Laura. What kind of alternate universe was she in? Where Laura was the one doing the saving?

They sat up, and Belle touched his face. "Thank you. I'll see you in the morning."

"Okay."

Belle stood and motioned for Laura to walk with her. "Come on. I'll help you find your room." She looked over her shoulder as Tristan stood. He smiled and winked. Even when she was exhausted, he could make her heart pound.

"Thanks, I'm sorry I interrupted," Laura said.

"It's okay." Not really. Not that they needed to be kissing, but Laura was invading her life, even after agreeing to leave her alone. It was like the universe was aligned against her. Forgiving her would be hard, especially when she couldn't trust her.

It was a pleasant surprise when Laura didn't try to chat her up. Instead, they walked quietly to her room, and then Belle went to hers. Telling Tristan what happened had helped. She felt lighter and more at peace than she had in a while.

CHAPTER 8

*U*ncomfortable silence hung in the air as Belle and Laura sat together in the glass-bottom boat. Laura had begged her to sightsee with her, but Belle stood firm. For once, she thought the universe was smiling down on her, but no. Somehow Laura found out Tristan wanted to snorkel and booked the last two spots on their outing.

Tristan had been sweet. He'd been willing to forgo snorkeling if it meant she didn't have to be around Laura, but she couldn't do that to him. He loved snorkeling, and it was his vacation too. He was already doing her a favor by pretending to date her.

Now, she wished she'd taken him up on his offer. Belle couldn't swim, and Laura had stayed behind instead of going out in the water with the group.

"Belle," Laura said, breaking the silence. "I know you don't want to talk to me, but I really want to talk to you."

Belle's shoulders drooped, and she hung her head. "Please leave me alone, Laura."

"Belle, please. I'm sorry. Are you ever going to forgive me?"

That was a big question. One she'd been struggling with since everything had happened, and even more so the moment she saw Laura on the cruise. How do you forgive someone you don't trust? Is forgiving them letting them off the hook? Or was it like her mom would say when she was a kid, that forgiveness wasn't for the person who wronged you. It was for yourself.

"I don't know. It's like you don't even comprehend what you did."

"I swear I do. What I did was awful and horrible. You have every right to hate me forever."

Belle looked at Laura. Typical. How many times had she heard that?

"That's the problem. I don't hate you. I should. I want to, but I don't." She sure wanted to hate Laura. Why *didn't* she hate her? Because it was hard to hate someone when it so easy to remember loving them.

"Please forgive me."

"I don't know how to forgive you yet. You really hurt me, Laura. We've known each other since we were juniors in high school, and you chose a guy over me." The knife in her heart, the one she thought she'd tossed, slipped back into its familiar spot.

Her friend's mouth curved down, and she looked like a balloon with a hole in it. "I know. It was wrong, but I can't time travel. I can't change what happened. If I could, I swear I would. All I can do is tell you I'm sorry. From the bottom of my heart, I'm sorry."

"And yet, you're still with Paul. He's not a good man. He's manipulative, cruel, and vindictive. We were competing for the same account, and he didn't just take it from me, he destroyed my career." Whoa. That had come out all at once. She hadn't meant to put it out there like that, but it was true. And if there was any chance of them being friends again, it had to be addressed.

Laura took her hand. "We've talked a lot about what happened, and he's sorry too. The pressure got to him. He wishes he could take it back."

"Is he sorry about the previous time he did it? That's why he was pushed out of his last agency. It was the same situation. He broke into their computer and did the same things to them." Belle was done holding back. If Laura married Paul, she'd at least go into it knowing who she was marrying.

Her friend shook her head. "That's not true. He told me what happened at that agency. They were jealous. He was doing well, and the owner's son was being petty by spreading rumors about him."

"So, I'm lying; is that it?" Of course she'd defend him. Same story, second verse.

"No, I just don't think you have all the facts."

"Okay, well, we're at the same place we were when all of it first happened. You trust him, and you don't trust me." She wasn't backing down. If Laura was going to take Paul's word over hers, she was going to do it without Belle helping her.

Laura's eyes went wide. "No, no. I just love you both. I want you both in my life. I love him, Belle. He's so good to me." She sniffed. "I shouldn't have done what I did. I know I shouldn't have, but I love him more than I've ever loved anyone."

Belle's stomach soured. It was nauseating to hear that coming from her lips. "Fine, but I will never trust him. He's not my friend. I don't like him, and being friends with me means understanding that."

"So you'll never give him another chance?" Laura asked as Paul broke through the surface of the water.

"No." That was as clear cut as she could put it.

"But we can be friends?"

"I don't know, but I'll answer your calls from now on."

Laura hugged her as Paul pulled himself onto the boat. "It looks like you two have made up. That's good."

Belle glared at him and then looked away. No, she'd never like him, trust him, or be friends with him, but she would be there when he broke Laura's heart, because she knew what that felt like.

Paul stopped in front of her, and she stood to put distance between them. When she did, he grabbed her by the waist and picked her up. "You should cool off."

"What? No. Let me go." Panic surged in her, and tears formed in her eyes. "Please, don't."

"Let her go, Paul. Can't you see she's scared?" Laura asked.

Paul laughed and said, "What better way to overcome your fears than facing them."

In a flash, the wind was knocked out of her as she hit the water with a scream. Water burned as it gushed up her nose. Her head popped up just long enough for her to gulp a bit of air, and down she went again. Despite her best effort to tread water, she could feel herself sinking.

TRISTAN WAS on his way back to the boat when he heard Belle scream, and then her body hit the water. All he could think was that she couldn't swim. He had to get to her. In a few good strokes, he was wrapping his arm around her waist and swimming to the surface.

Belle clung to him, coughing and choking. Her tiny body trembled.

He ripped the snorkel off and tossed it into the boat. "It's okay. You're safe." She almost wasn't, and the thought made his chest tighten. "Let's get you on the boat."

Laura took her and pulled her up, and Tristan hauled himself up right behind her. Belle immediately locked her arms around his neck and cried.

He looked at Laura. "What happened? She can't swim, so why was she in the water?"

Laura wrung her hands together. "Paul was trying to be funny. He thought she could swim."

"I swear I did. I was just trying to joke around."

Tristan balled his hands into fists. "Don't you ever touch her again."

Paul held his hands up. "Lighten up. I was just trying to have a little fun."

He'd never been so angry in his life. "It wasn't funny, and I'm not kidding. Put your hands on her again, and I'll pound you into the pavement." Then he looked at Laura and bit his tongue.

She and Belle were still working through things, and he didn't want to come between them. But he didn't like Laura. Belle deserved a better friend, but until she came to that decision, there was no point in saying anything.

Tristan took Belle to the other end of the boat and sat down with her in his lap. "Are you okay?"

"I think so." Her arms tightened around him.

"Think you can loosen the grip? I think my face is turning purple." He chuckled.

She slowly let go and pulled back. "I'm sorry."

"I was kidding. You hold on to me however tightly you need to." The adrenaline began to wear off. It had been heart-stopping scary for him, so he could only imagine how bad it was for her.

A tiny laugh came from her. "If you hadn't been here…"

"But I was, and you're safe. And I meant what I said. If he touches you again, I'm going to get kicked off the boat for decking him." And possibly sued.

"You're turning out to be my knight in shining armor. Pretending to be my boyfriend, speaking up when I don't have words, and saving my life, all in the span of four days." She held his gaze. "Thank you."

Tristan shook his head. "I'm sure I'll need rescuing soon."

"Um, I'm sorry about that," Laura said as she approached.

He was still furious. There was no excuse for what Paul had done and even less of an excuse for Laura to defend him. "She needs some space."

Laura nodded and walked back to the other end of the boat.

He needed to do something to make her smile. "How about I book you a massage?"

"Oh, no, I couldn't accept that. You kept me from drowning. I'd say you've done your good deed."

"It's my fault you were on the boat in the first place. I should have found something else to do the moment I found out you couldn't swim. And definitely after Laura and Paul showed up."

Belle smiled. "I'm a big girl, Tristan. I wanted to go. The boat was great, and I got to see some really cool things."

"I know you are, but this isn't for you. It's for me. Let me do this, okay?"

She looked down. "I don't know. You've already

been really nice to me. I feel like I'd be taking advantage of you."

For a second, he was floored. She didn't want to take advantage of him. "You aren't." He hooked a finger under her chin and make her look at him. "Please?"

"Okay." She held his face and kissed his cheek. "You are the sweetest man I've ever met."

Tristan wanted to kiss her so badly it hurt. He shook the thought away. They were friends. That's what they both wanted. Instead, he held her until the boat hit the sand.

Tristan returned his rented snorkeling gear and took Belle to the spa. After they decided on a time to meet up later in front of the open-air market a few blocks over, Tristan decided to explore on his own. Maybe he'd find something for her. Something small she could keep with her that would let her remember Grand Turk for more than nearly drowning.

It was insane. He was insane. Four days in, and he was behaving like a schoolboy with a crush. He never thought it was possible, but he'd never met anyone like Belle, either. At this rate, who knew what day nine would bring.

CHAPTER 9

*O*f course, the moment Tristan had dropped Belle off at the spa for her massage, Laura had shown up. It was as though Belle couldn't get a moment away from her. Why did Laura have to keep pushing herself on her?

She couldn't ask for a different time slot either. They were only on Grand Turk for so long, and she wanted to sightsee a little.

"Oh, this feels so good," Laura groaned. She'd insisted that they take the massage together, and not wanting to cause a scene, Belle had reluctantly agreed.

Belle had to admit, the massage was great. Muscles she didn't even know she had were having the tension slowly kneaded away. "Yeah."

"Tell me about Tristan."

Tristan. His name was like honey in her mouth. Mentally, she balked at telling Laura anything about him. The feeling was so fierce it caused her pulse to jump. Where did it come from? She was just asking a simple question. It was what friends did. Did she see Laura as a friend now?

"You don't have to if you don't want to." The sadness in her voice pulled at Belle's heart.

It was casual talk. She could tell Laura what she thought of Tristan. "He's sweet, kind, protective, and caring. He's wonderful."

"What do you know about him?" Laura asked.

Did she want to share any of this with Laura? Would Tristan be okay with it being shared? "He was raised by his grandmother." He was pretty open with that, so that felt safe. She'd warn him when they met up again.

"What else?"

"He lives in Seattle, but he's traveled a lot."

Laura pushed up on her elbows. "Belle, I don't think he's being honest with you. I think there's more to him than you know."

Anger flooded her. "And you're one to talk about that?"

"He wore a six-thousand-dollar suit to dinner last night. I know because when Paul and I were in New

York, we stopped in at Barney's. That suit was some fancy designer like Brioni or something. And his swim trunks were three-hundred-dollar Thorson's. How does a regular person afford that?" Laura knitted her eyebrows together. "I just...who is he?"

His suit was crazy good-looking on him, and the trunks fit him perfectly. His dark olive skin against the white of the shorts made him exotic eye candy. Who cares if he had money. What if he'd inherited it or something? What did it matter? "So what? He wears expensive clothing. His money doesn't make him who he is. I don't need to know everything about him to know he's a good person."

Laura laid her head back down. "Okay, I'm sorry. He is sweet, and he obviously cares about you. You should have seen the way he looked at Paul. If you hadn't been holding on to him, I think he'd have really hurt Paul."

Would have served him right. Jerk. Big, fat, stupid jerk. She'd nearly drowned. But then Tristan had come to her rescue like a superhero. She could still feel his arms around her. "We're good friends, and I like that."

"Good friends? I'd say you're more than that. You're dating."

"Well, yeah, but we're friends too." Belle wanted

her to stop talking so she could relax. It was a massage, after all, and talking didn't help ease the tension.

"Okay. How is your mom doing?"

Belle pushed up on her elbows and looked at Laura. "She's in the best nursing facility in Miami. Winning this cruise let me pay ahead and make sure she stays there. Money's been a little tight." Laura didn't need to know anything about her job or what she was doing.

"You could've called me. You know I'd help."

She lay back down. "No, I needed to take care of it myself." Calling Laura hadn't been an option. The fact that she was at a spa with her made her feel weird and uncomfortable. Laura had been her best friend, and the last few months she'd struggled with being on her own. Which is why she cherished her blossoming friendship with Tristan and didn't want to ruin it.

"I'm glad she's somewhere good. I know the last place was awful."

Yeah, the last place had been one step up from a nightmare. Glory Blooms was a godsend. They had fantastic nurses, great food, and onsite round-the-clock doctors. Belle was eating peanut butter and jelly sandwiches, but her mom was getting the best care, for once. "I was worried about moving her to Miami, but it's been a good change. On the days when she's doing well, she talks about how great it is."

"That's so great."

"I think so too."

"You think we could visit her when the ship docks back in Miami?"

Laura was trying too hard, but she did know her mom. "I guess so."

"Thanks." Laura pushed up on her elbows again. "Okay, so, it's been a while. Have you seen what Angelina Jolie is up to?"

"Nope. Don't care." She knew that wouldn't shut her up, but it would allow her to mumble "uh-huh" for the next hour. And that's exactly what happened.

She'd keep Laura's invasion to herself. Tristan had meant for her to enjoy her massage, and telling him would only bother him because she'd been trapped with Laura yet again.

"HEY." Belle smiled, lifted on her toes, and kissed Tristan on the cheek. "Miss me?" Her bag hung on her shoulder, and she wore a floral spaghetti strap dress with simple sandals. She was adorable as usual.

She was joking, but he *had* missed her. "Yeah, I did. I got you something."

Her lips parted, and she looked at him bewildered. "What? You already got me a massage. That was more than enough."

He handed her the small gift bag. "Yeah, but I saw it and thought of you."

"You didn't have to do that. I just like being with you." She slapped a hand over her mouth. "I mean, you really didn't have to do that."

Tristan had never gotten a response like that. "I know. Open it."

She set her bag down and pulled out the little box. When she opened it, she gasped and pulled out the little jeweled ring. "Oh, Tristan, it's beautiful. I love it."

"I did say it reminded me of you." In his world, it was practically free, and given to any of the women he'd dated before, it would have been rejected. Not her. The look on her face spread warmth through him. She didn't care about the gift at all. She appreciated it and valued it, but by the way she looked at him, he meant more to her than the gift.

He took a deep breath. Friends. They were friends. That's all she wanted. He needed to remember that. She was sweet and appreciative of things. Nothing more.

She slipped the ring on her index finger and splayed her hand in the sun. "Look how it sparkles. It's so pretty."

Laura walked up with Paul's arm around her shoulders. Those two were determined to steal all their time together. "Oh, that's cute."

"Tristan gave it to me. It's perfect."

Perfect? Hardly, but her smile was worth every penny. "It was just a trinket."

"The best trinket." She kissed him. "Thank you. You're so sweet."

For a moment, he forgot it wasn't real. His racing heart skidded to a stop and his head dropped out of the clouds. This was a fake relationship. It was getting harder to remember that.

Laura took her hand and looked at Tristan. "That was really thoughtful."

Paul narrowed his eyes at Tristan and then grinned. He pulled out a velvet box and knelt down. "I got you something too."

Laura's hands flew to her mouth with a gasp. "Oh, Paul, but I already have a ring."

"Yeah, but this one's bigger." He winked at her.

Tristan could have thrown up, and by the looks of Belle, she could've too.

Belle stepped closer to Tristan and laced her

fingers with his. She tiptoed and whispered, "He's just trying to outdo you. What he doesn't know is that he can't."

If she only knew who he really was. What he could really afford. Paul's grand gesture would look more like a trinket than the ring he'd given Belle. Even from where he stood, he could tell it was a fake diamond.

"Laura Denning, would you do me the pleasure of making me the happiest man alive and marry me?" Quicker than Laura could see, Paul cut his eyes to Belle. He really was a snake. Well, both of them were, or that's what Tristan thought. There was something off about Laura. He hoped Belle would figure it out soon, before she got hurt again.

Belle leaned in again. "I hope you won't be mad, but Laura asked me about you earlier. All I told her was that you were raised by your grandma. I hope that's okay. I didn't say anything else."

"It's okay." He tucked a piece of her hair behind her ear, and she leaned her face into his hand.

Laura grabbed Belle and hugged her. "Isn't it gorgeous? It catches the sun and glitters."

"Yeah, it's great, but I thought you were already engaged," she said, looking at Paul.

He shrugged. "Yeah, but I figured why not splurge."

Tristan coughed. It'd almost come out as a laugh.

Splurge? This guy was a piece of work. "My throat's dry. Maybe we could grab a drink and celebrate."

They walked a few doors down and found a beachy-looking cantina filled with weathered picnic tables and benches. Old street signs, pictures of celebrities, and flyers for local bands littered the walls. They sat at a table on the far side of the room, and a waitress took their drink order.

"So, Tristan," Laura said as the waitress left. "What do you do for a living?"

How did he answer that question without lying? If it was just him and Belle, he might be willing to divulge who he was. "I do a little bit of everything, really." It was true. The businesses he bought and turned around were varied, from investment to real estate and everything in between.

"Like what?"

"Real estate, construction, a little bit of finance." That was as much as they were getting from him.

Paul narrowed his eyes. "Finance?"

"Yes, a little."

He nodded and seemed to let it go, but Tristan got a weird feeling from him.

When Laura's drink arrived in a pineapple, he grinned as he thought of Grayson with one in his hand.

"Belle tells me you were raised by your grandmother," Laura said and set her drink down. "You must be really close with her."

Speaking of her in the present tense momentarily winded him. "Was. She died about three months ago after being ill the prior eight months."

Under the table, Belle covered his hand with hers and leaned into him.

"I'm so sorry. Do you have any other family?" Laura asked.

"I have an aunt, but she's all I have left." Tristan could hear the melancholy in his voice. Other than Aunt Felicia and Grayson, he was alone in the world. Not alone; he had other friends. They were just the only ones he trusted implicitly.

Belle took a deep breath and said, "Do you have everything ready for the wedding?"

How much did it hurt for her to do that? To take the attention from him and talk about something she was struggling with. She had an incredible amount of strength and courage.

Laura brightened and sat forward. "Yes. I have my dress, the place, the minister, everything. Does this mean you'll be my maid of honor?"

The hesitation was slight, and she stiffened. "I don't

know yet, but I haven't ruled it out completely at this point."

Tristan was in awe of her. She'd given Laura a carrot so the conversation would move away from him. Emotionally, she'd pushed him out of the line of fire.

For the first time in his life, a woman cared about him. Not his name, his money, or what she could gain from being with him; she cared about him. What was he going to do when being friends with her wasn't enough anymore?

He shook his head to clear the crazy thought. It was going to be enough. He'd make sure it was enough. Belle wasn't looking for a relationship. She'd been straight with him from the beginning. This trip would end, and they'd end it as friends.

CHAPTER 10

Maritsa skipped over to Belle as she and Tristan stopped in front of their room doors. "Hey, guys. Marketing wants to get a few photos of us, so Ashley, Shawn, and I are going to play pool. We insist you two come with us. We just don't want Belle playing," she said and laughed loudly.

"Hey, I warned all of you I couldn't play. That I was dangerous even. It's not my fault you didn't take me seriously." Belle grinned. "Let me get changed, and I'll hang out. I'm sure you three have some great stories to tell, right?"

It was late. She was tired, but she knew she wouldn't be able to sleep just yet. She'd given Laura hope that she'd agree to be in her wedding. Her plan had been to tell her no. Flat-out no, not a chance.

Then the questions came about Tristan's grandmother, and she knew that was the only way Laura would drop it.

Maritsa wiggled her eyebrows. "What's a cruise without horror stories and harrowing adventures?"

"I'll be right out." She paused at her door and glanced at Tristan.

He looked troubled. Much like he had since they'd had drinks at the cantina.

"See you two in a second." Maritsa spun on her heel and bounced away.

Tristan waited until Maritsa was out of sight and followed Belle inside her room. "I'll see you in a second too. I need to change. I'm thinking a shower and my other set of runway pajamas." She winked.

"Wait. I..." He paused and looked torn about something. "What you did earlier today was above and beyond anything anyone has ever done for me. At least in recent years. I know it hurt you to bring up her wedding. You didn't have to do that."

"It's okay. I couldn't let the questions about your family continue. If Laura had kept going, Paul would have used it as an opportunity to hurt you. It's not a big deal. It's not like I've said yes. In Laura's mind I have, but I haven't." She smiled up at him.

"Yes, but now she'll be hounding you even more

because she thinks you're going to give in. You didn't have to do that." He looked at her in disbelief.

Belle waved him off. "It was nothing. Really. At least this way, you didn't have to deal with their prying questions. Laura only thinks she's going to get what she wants. At this point, nothing is set in stone, so don't worry about it." She reached up and kissed his cheek. "Now, go get changed. We're going to play some pool and relax. Well, you'll play; I'll watch."

"Okay, I'll see you in the game lounge in fifteen?"

"Yep."

She shut the door behind Tristan as he left and leaned against it. If he'd stayed any longer, she'd have ended up kissing him. The ring he'd given her was beautiful and made her feel special. He was quickly becoming her favorite person.

A little voice piped up, whispering things she wasn't ready to hear, and she shoved them back down. He was different than Paul, and she knew it. But that didn't mean her heart was ready to take another chance. She could be falling for him, but she wouldn't fall. Even if she had to shackle herself to the edge of the cliff.

Twenty minutes later, Belle was in the game room with Maritsa, Ashley, Shawn, and Tristan as they played pool. Setting her elbow on the bar table, she put her head in her hand as her thoughts drifted to Laura. Belle had nearly drowned, and Laura had the gall to come to Paul's defense? As if there was one. Then she'd forced herself on Belle at the spa and run her mouth the entire hour.

"You okay?" Tristan asked.

"Yeah," she said. The answer came out a little more forced than she intended.

He chuckled. "You've been grumbling to yourself for the last two hours."

"It's been two hours?"

"I'm afraid so."

Belle sighed. "I just can't stop thinking about Laura. I'm so angry with her. I don't want to be, but I am."

"Maybe I can help with that." The look he gave her said he knew exactly what she was going through.

He returned his pool stick to the cue rack and took Belle's hand. "Hey, guys, we're going to call it a night."

"Aww, we're just getting started," Maritsa said.

Belle slid off the barstool and faked a yawn. "Yep, don't want to be a zombie in San Juan tomorrow."

Once they said their goodnights, they grabbed a few blankets and found a lounge chair on the deck. It had become one of her favorite things. Just sitting on the deck, talking to a friend. Her heart stammered, and she mentally flicked it with her fingers.

"I know what it's like to be angry," Tristan said. "It's a hard thing to work through because you think being angry is the only way to feel like you've gotten justice."

She nodded as he put his arms around her and drew her close. "I don't want to be angry, but I am. I'm sick of this pattern I have with her. I'm sick of her treating me however she wants. Of always doing things and expecting me to forgive her and then acting like nothing ever happened."

"When I lost my parents, my dad was the pilot flying the plane when it crashed. I blamed him, even though I was told it wasn't his fault. I went to live with my grandma, and I was really angry. I was pulled from my school, taken from my home, and though I was living with someone I loved, she wasn't my mom and dad. I was mad at my parents. I was mad at the accident. I was mad at my grandma. I was angry with the world."

Belle had a hard time picturing Tristan being like that. He was so kind and loving. "I have trouble believing that."

"Believe it. I acted out in my new school, got in trouble constantly, argued with my grandmother. I did awful things to her. Plugging toilets, toilet papering neighbors' homes—it was an upscale gated community. Needless to say, my grandma had to do a lot to save face when I did that. I did anything and everything I could to make everyone around me miserable."

She chuckled. "Okay, now you sound like a little terror."

"I was for a few years. Until I realized that the only person who was miserable was me. I loved my new school. It had a great basketball team, and I had more friends than I'd ever had before. I loved my grandmother's home, especially my room. She'd given me this room filled with all sorts of surfing memorabilia. I was really into surfing when I was a kid, and she'd done it just for me. To make me feel more at home." He swallowed hard and when he spoke again, his voice was husky. "Most of all, I loved my grandmother. She put up with a lot. She didn't have to raise another child, but she did."

Belle didn't know what to say. It had to hurt to stir up all those memories, and he was doing it to help her.

"Letting go of anger and bitterness…it's for yourself. It's so you can move on and be happy. You deserve to be happy, Belle. Why let someone who doesn't care about you dictate your happiness?"

"How did you do it?"

Tristan shrugged. "When I was fifteen, I got into really big trouble. I stole a car and ended up wrecking it. Luckily, no one was hurt, but I will never forget how my grandma looked at me or the grief in her voice when she told me she was disappointed in me. I felt lower than low. My grandmother was hurt, but I was the one who was miserable."

"What happened?"

"After she bailed me out, we had a long talk. My grandmother told me I needed to forgive my parents. She said she'd been angry too, but being angry with them wouldn't bring them back, that living in misery wasn't what they would have wanted for either of us. Wrecking the car wasn't the smartest thing I could have done, but it woke me up.

"Over the next year, I worked off the debt for the car. I went to school, brought my grades up, and treated my grandmother with the respect she was due. By the time I turned sixteen, I was a different person. It took me a long time to forgive myself though. There are times I still have to do it."

"So, what you're saying is that if stop being angry and forgive Laura, I'll be happier?"

"I'm saying you should consider it. I'm not saying she deserves it, by any means. I honestly don't know why you were friends with her in the first place, but if you're going to move on and find peace, you'll have to let the anger go. Forgiving her is your call."

Belle took a deep breath and laid her head against

his chest. It was a lot to digest. She'd said she didn't want to be angry, but it had proven to be impossible. How was she supposed to do it? Just say, "I'm not angry anymore"? Did it work like that?

"How do I do it?"

He combed his fingers down the length of her hair. "I made a conscious decision to stop being angry, and then I followed through. The moment I did, it was like being freed from a personal jail."

Just how badly did she want to be happy? Was it worth it letting go of her anger towards Laura? "I don't want to be angry anymore. I'm exhausted."

Without saying anything, Tristan put his arms around her and held her tightly. They spent the next few hours quietly lying on the lounge together, watching the stars. By the time they went to their rooms, Belle had silently made a choice.

She was done being angry, and Tristan was right. It was like being freed from a cell. She felt light and happy for the first time in—she couldn't remember how long. It made her wish she'd done it sooner.

"You look tired. Did you not sleep?" asked Laura.

Belle yawned for the umpteenth time and rubbed

her face with her hands. "A few of the passengers we met the first day asked Tristan and me to play pool last night in the game lounge."

The evening before, Laura had begged Belle to have breakfast with her before exploring San Juan. Only, it was just the two of them. It felt weird to have Laura sitting across from her after so many months of being on her own.

The previous night played in her mind. Tristan had been so open. She would have never guessed he'd ever been that angry. A stolen car? Nope, she couldn't see him doing that at all. And with the way he spoke of his grandma, she couldn't picture him ever treating her with anything but respect. She'd decided she was going to be done being angry, but her feathers had ruffled the moment Laura had come into view.

Her friend's eyes grew wide as saucers. "Were there injuries?"

"Shut up. I didn't play. I watched." A laugh escaped. It was the first real laugh she'd had with Laura since she found about her and Paul. Maybe there was a chance they could be friends again. Maybe it could be repaired. Not right away, but maybe it could move in that direction. Despite not wanting to, Belle had missed Laura. The thought brought tears to her eyes, and she looked down at her plate.

Maybe emptying herself of the pain, hurt, and anger would give her what she really wanted: her friend. Even if that meant waiting for Paul to break her heart. Paul was using her, Belle knew it. He'd manipulated her, and men had always been Laura's weakness. Her desperation to be loved made her an easy target.

Belle squeezed her eyes shut. If she told Laura it was done and over, Laura would expect things to be the way they were. She would expect her to be the maid of honor at her wedding. Could she handle that? Was she ready? Her heart hammered in her chest, and her stomach churned.

Laura's wedding was the next day. Agreeing to be her maid of honor didn't have to mean they were best buddies again. It could be a symbol that she was allowing herself to be free. Forgiving her was not forgetting what happened, it was letting go of the hurt and anger. It didn't mean they had to be friends.

"Are you okay?" Laura's voice brought her out of her thoughts.

Was she okay? "I think so."

Maybe she was too tired to be thinking about these things. What if she woke up tomorrow and regretted everything she said today? But what if she woke up tomorrow, feeling better than she had in months?

Belle stretched her arm across the table and took Laura's hand. "I forgive you."

"Really? Like forgive, forgive, or you'll just tolerate me now?" Laura's large brown eyes pierced her heart.

"Forgiven, totally and completely." Belle was sure she'd have to choke out the words, but she didn't. They flowed out like they'd been waiting to be released. "You should thank Tristan. He's the reason I'm doing it."

Laura covered Belle's hand with hers. "Then, I'll thank him. And thank you. I know I don't deserve it."

No, she didn't. She held back the part where she didn't trust her. With time, maybe they'd get back to that too. "If we got what we deserve, we'd all be in trouble." Belle gave her a small smile. "I'm not saying I won't trip up and say something I shouldn't, but I do forgive you."

A tear streaked down Laura's cheek. "That's okay. I'll take it."

Belle changed seats and hugged Laura. "I've missed you. I can't believe you're getting married."

Laura leaned back and looked at her with big teary eyes. "Does forgiving me mean you'll be my maid of honor?"

"Yeah, I'll be your maid of honor."

She crushed her in a hug and cried. "I've missed

you so much. I didn't want to get married without you there."

Belle pulled back. "Don't get mad at me, okay?"

Laura rubbed her nose with a napkin and nodded. "Okay."

"Be honest with me and yourself. Does Paul treat you the way you want to be treated?" Belle knew it was a risk, but the question would have bored a hole in her brain if she hadn't asked.

A pause. It was slight, but it was there. "Yeah, he does. I wouldn't be marrying him if he didn't."

"I know you probably think I only asked because I don't like him, but I don't want to see you get hurt. I had to ask." She hoped Laura understood.

"I know, and we wouldn't be us if you didn't." Laura hugged her again. "You don't know how much I needed this."

"Yeah, I do, because I needed it just as much." The world slid off her shoulders, and she felt light enough to float.

Footfalls behind them made them let go and turn. "Hey." Laura stood and hugged Paul around the neck.

Tristan eyed Belle and bent down. "You okay?"

"Actually, yeah. I did something for me," she said.

He looked at her, puzzled. "What?"

"I forgave her." She hadn't felt so free in months.

His lips brushed across her cheek and stopped at her ear. "You are a special person, Belle Evans."

Her eyes slid closed, and she leaned into him. "You keep doing that, and I might be forced to kiss you here in the middle of the dining pavilion." She jerked back. When did she start blurting stuff out? He was turning her brain into mush.

When she looked at him, he winked.

Belle swatted him on the arm. "That's not fair."

"I know," he said and chuckled.

"You ready to explore San Juan?" She pushed his hair off his forehead and wanted nothing more than to be alone with him. Ugh. What was it about Tristan Davis that made her so gooey?

He shot her a look through a fringe of lashes, and if she hadn't been sitting down, she'd have fallen down. Talk about not fair. If there was a medal for sexy looks, he'd be taking home the gold, hands down. "As long as it's with you."

"You stop looking at me like that." She tapped his nose.

Tristan laughed as he straightened and stuffed his hands in the pockets of his shorts. "I'm ready to see San Juan."

Laura grinned. "Me too."

Paul curled his arm around Laura. "I've got us

booked for a horseback ride on the beach." He looked at Tristan and Belle. "I hope you guys don't mind, but I'd like a few hours alone with her today."

"No, not at all." Belle said. At least she wouldn't have to see his stupid face for the rest of the day.

Laura took her hand. "We'll meet up with you when the ride is over. You guys need to do something romantic too."

Tristan tangled his fingers in her free hand and winked at her. "We'll figure out something."

He was downright swoon-worthy. "Cut that out."

Laura giggled, and she and Paul said their good-byes. Just before they left, Laura turned to Tristan and said, "Thank you."

He gave a little nod but didn't say anything until after they were gone. "I'm serious about finding something to do. I bet there's all sorts of trouble we can get into." He smiled.

She yawned. "I shouldn't have stayed up so late. I feel groggy."

His fingertips trailed across her cheeks, and she leaned in. "We can also just stay on the ship and relax."

That sounded more like the "all sorts of trouble" he was talking about. "No, Laura's right. We can go to San Juan and do a walking tour or something. Maybe do window shopping or sit on the beach and play guess the yacht price."

His warm laughter made her want to cuddle up to him and find a quiet place to kiss. "Sounds like a plan. Do you need to get anything? Your purse?"

"No, it's not like I could spend anything anyway. I'll just be looking. Besides, I have my ring you gave me. That's enough." She smiled.

"Then let's go."

CHAPTER 11

A walking tour with Belle was entirely different than a walking tour with any of the women he'd dated in the past. She actually listened to the guide and seemed genuinely interested in the tour. Never once did she whine about it taking too long or indicate that she'd rather be shopping.

"Isn't this great?" She covered her mouth as she yawned. "I'm sorry. I am listening, but I'm so sleepy. I will not be staying up that late again. If I'm not tired, I'm going to count sheep or something."

Tristan twisted his finger around a strand of her hair. "The only reason I'm enjoying this tour is because I'm with you. I like how your eyes sparkle in the sun."

She lightly smacked his arm. "I said stop that. I can't afford new headbands."

He enjoyed her humor, how down to earth she was. She didn't expect compliments or demand them. Belle was just Belle. "I don't think that's possible to stop."

Her lips curved up into a smile. "Whatever. This is almost over. What do you want to do next?"

What could they do next? There had to be something interesting to do on the island. "How about we just wander through the market?"

"Okay. Are you hungry? Because I'm kinda hungry. Oh geez, I'm so stupid. Let me get my purse from the ship. I wasn't kidding when I said I was sleepy. I wasn't thinking about needing money for lunch." Her strawberry blonde hair danced around her shoulders as she shook her head like she was trying to wake herself up.

Before she could take off, Tristan stopped her. "My treat."

"No, I can pay my own way. We'll just have to find somewhere not too expensive. I'm ahead on payments to the nursing home, but I don't want to go crazy spending." She slapped a hand over her mouth. "Uh, I'm sorry. Um, I'll go get my purse."

He tightened his grip on her wrist. "Nursing

home?" That's right. He remembered her mentioning that now.

"It's nothing. Come on; I'll get my purse." She pulled on him to walk with her.

"I pay, or you tell me about the nursing home." Why was she paying for a nursing home? Tristan thought back to Laura. Her mom? She was too young to have a parent in a nursing home.

She chewed her thumb as her eyes darted back and forth. "You can pay, and I'll pay you back."

"Okay." He reluctantly agreed, but he did want to know the story behind the nursing home.

They finished the walking tour and meandered through the downtown streets until they found a little hole-in-the-wall selling sandwiches. With their orders in hand, they found a spot on the sidewalk patio and sat down. She'd ordered the cheapest thing on the menu, even after he insisted it was okay and he didn't mind buying them lunch.

"This is good," she said and wiped her mouth with a napkin. "Have you been here before?"

"Why would you think I've been here before?" he asked. He wasn't sure why, but the question struck him wrong. Had she somehow figure out who he was and was trying to catch him in his lie? Had she been faking this whole time, acting like she didn't know who he really was?

She shrugged. "You said you were transient and had been to the Caribbean a few times. You seemed to know your way around, and I was curious."

Tristan narrowed his eyes. "What?" She did know. How had he been so blind? He thought he'd found someone who cared about him. Just him. Not his name or his money, but she was no different from all the rest. He'd been baring his heart to her, and all this time, she'd been using him too.

"I don't know. You just seem to have a familiarity with the place."

He stiffened. "Have you been researching me?" How many times had it happened? Women pretending they didn't know him, just to find out they were lying. He thought Belle was different. She seemed different. Genuine. He'd been so stupid. She was just another woman willing to go any length for money. Anger and betrayal burned in the pit of his stomach.

"What?" Her eyebrows knitted together, and she looked at him curiously.

All the times he'd been used by people floated through his mind. "You heard me. I thought you liked me for me, but you did a search. You know who I am. That's why you left your purse on the ship. You knew

I'd pay." His voice had risen, and the people around were beginning to stare. He wasn't sure what had come over him. Belle was different. She had to be. Didn't she?

She reached across the table for his hand, and he jerked it back. "You don't have to tell me who you are, and I swear I'll pay you back."

It was irrational anger. She'd ordered the cheapest thing on the menu. She'd insisted on paying, and he was the one who wouldn't let her go get her purse. Still, his mind couldn't stop the thought that maybe she'd played him like all the other women.

His heart was on the floor. His grandmother was wrong. There was no way to find someone who would love him. Not when all they could see was his money.

"I think we're done." He wiped his mouth, stood, and shoved his chair under the table.

She raced after him as he walked away and stopped him. "Tristan, what did I do? I'm sorry. Don't go. I'll get my purse and pay you right now."

"I need some space. Just stick the money under my door." He brushed past her and walked at least a mile before he stopped.

He had no idea what had come over him. She'd done nothing wrong. It was a simple question, but he'd lost it. It was stupid. What he needed to do was turn around immediately and beg for forgiveness. But his feet wouldn't budge. Ducking into an almost empty bar, he pulled out his phone and dialed Grayson.

"Hey! It's about time. How's that head of yours?" Grayson asked.

Not screwed on tight enough. "It's okay, I guess. How are things?"

"Nothing new to report. Last board meeting was basically bickering and whining that you weren't there."

Tristan raked a hand through his hair. "So, *really* nothing new to report. They'd just whine if I was there."

"This is true." Grayson paused. "Why are you calling me? Have you met someone? Don't tell me you've already screwed it up."

"I lost it a few minutes ago."

"Lost it? Where are you?"

"San Juan."

"And you left me here? You're a complete jerk. You know that?" Grayson's voice ticked up an octave.

"Yeah, in more ways than one," he murmured.

"What did you do?"

Should he tell Grayson what he was doing? That he'd hidden on board his grandmother's ship and was pretending to be someone else? It was the only way for any of it to make sense, so Tristan gave him the short version. Then he filled him in on what had just happened with Belle.

"So, this woman doesn't know who you are?"

"No, I'm pretty sure she doesn't."

"And you flipped out on her because she asked if you'd been to San Juan before?"

"Yeah."

"Idiot."

Leave it to Grayson to point out the obvious. "Yeah."

"Go back. Tell her you're sorry for being a complete moron. Make it up to her."

"I can't."

"Why not?"

"I don't know. I liked the idea that she didn't know who I am. That I'm not just a dollar sign to her. The thought that she might have figured it out bugs me."

"Has she acted like she cares about money at all?"

Actually, she hadn't behaved in a way that even suggested she cared about money. "Not even a little bit. She wanted to pay me back for a five-dollar sandwich."

"Tristan, man, I love you, but you need to fix this. It sounds like you might have found a woman who cares about you. Go. Fix it. Who cares if she knows who you are. She'll find out eventually if you keep seeing her."

Seeing her? That wasn't exactly the case, but he did like being friends with her. "I know, but..."

"You said she doesn't care about the money, right?"

"Yeah. Doesn't seem to."

"Well, telling her you're Tristan Stone isn't going to change anything except she'll know your last name."

Grayson was right. In his heart, he knew Belle cared about him. She'd protected him even when it cost her. What had caused him to panic?

He sank into a chair. The answer was so simple Tristan couldn't believe he'd missed it. He was terrified. Belle was kind to him. She saw him when no one else had. Deep down, he'd been waiting for it to crash at his feet, and at even the slightest suggestion that he might have been wrong about her, he ran. This time it wasn't a woman who had destroyed everything. It was him.

He needed to fix it. He only hoped she would give him a second chance.

"I'm an idiot."

"That, we can absolutely agree on, but it's kind of a running thing with you."

"Shut up."

"Fix it, man, before the chance is gone."

They said their goodbyes, and Tristan hurried out of the bar. Hopefully, Belle hadn't gotten too far and she would forgive him. He'd tell her who he was and explain. She'd listen. She always did.

LIGHTS PULSED as Belle perched on a barstool next to Laura that evening. She'd gone out of her way to avoid Tristan after he'd yelled at her on the sidewalk. When she got back to the ship, she'd slipped what she owed him under his door and then had gone to Laura's room to hide. Never in a million years would she have thought Laura would actually come to her rescue. She didn't want to see him, and it hurt like a paper cut.

"Thanks for doing this. It's so much fun. I know it's not the crazy bachelorette party I always talked about, but you're here. And I'm just glad we're friends again." Laura took a long sip of her drink.

At the moment, Belle didn't want to contradict her about the status of their friendship. She stared at Laura's drink. She had yet to order anything more than water. She didn't know why, but the idea of drinking turned her off for some reason. "Is it good?"

"This?" She pointed to the glass filled with different

colored alcoholic slushy mixes. "Delicious. You should get one. Tristan isn't here. Have a drink."

Tristan wasn't there. He wasn't ever going to be there again. He'd said he needed space. It's what Paul had said right before Laura confessed she'd been having an affair with him. Belle didn't get second chances. Life dealt the hand, and that's all there was to it.

"You're right." As a waiter passed by, she snagged him and ordered a drink.

Laura wiggled happily in her seat. "Yay! I'm not drinking alone now."

Three drinks later, Belle felt light-headed. "Thanks for this."

"Thanks for shopping with me today. And we found you a dress." Laura bumped her with her shoulder.

Belle had to admit it had been fun shopping with Laura, and the dress they found was pretty. It'd be great for her wedding the next day. It had also allowed her to avoid talking about Tristan.

"What happened with Tristan?" her friend asked.

Well, she'd avoided it until now. "It doesn't matter." It didn't. It was too good to be true, and deep down she knew that all along.

Laura pursed her lips and leaned over. "I'm sorry to see you so sad. I could tell you really liked him."

"It's okay."

"How long have you been dating him? Really?" Laura asked.

Belle grunted a laugh. "We're not. I only said that because I didn't want to look pathetic to Paul or you."

"What?"

"I'm pathetic. I know it. I should have just been honest from the start." Belle set her elbow on the table and put her head in it. "Being honest would have prevented this."

"Prevented what?"

"I'm falling for him. I'm drawn to him. His dark-brown eyes, his smile, the way he smells and walks. All of it. I flat out adore him." She couldn't believe she'd just said that aloud.

Laura nodded her head. "He's pretty dreamboaty. And he sure can dress."

"Yeah, he can. When he winks at me, my stomach just flutters and my palms sweat." A stab of pain hit her. "But it's over, and that's that."

Her somewhere-between-ex-friend-and-friend rubbed her back. "Let's just have a good time tonight, and we'll worry about what to do tomorrow."

Hours went by, and Belle ordered a few more

drinks. What did she care? Laura was paying, Tristan wasn't there, and she needed to be numb for a minute. Her mom, the nursing home, her crashed marketing career, a failed relationship, and now the man she was so drawn to it hurt to be away from him was done with her…It was more than she could handle.

Belle slipped off the barstool, staggered, and palmed her forehead. "Oh, I think I need to lie down."

Laura's shrill giggle made her ears ring.

"Oh, hey, honey," Laura said.

"Hi."

Belle looked up, and Paul was standing next to Laura.

"Are you drunk?" he asked.

She could lie, but it would be a pretty bad one. "Yep." As long as she held on to the table, she was fine. Letting go was the issue. How was she going to get to her room?

"Can you even walk?" Laura asked and giggled.

"I don't know." Belle's head and stomach hurt.

Paul touched her arm. "I'll help you."

"No, I can do it." She released the table, and Paul caught her before she hit the floor.

"No, you can't. Let me help you." He looked at Laura. "Stay here. I'll be back for you, okay?"

"I didn't drink as much as she did. I'll be fine."
Laura touched his arm. "Thank you."

Belle didn't want Paul doing anything for her. Even
as drunk as she was, she knew that. Alarm bells went
off in her head, but she was so dizzy they sounded like
a broken carousel. It *was* the night before his wedding.
He wouldn't do anything to jeopardize that, right? He
didn't even like her, so she shouldn't have anything to
be worried about.

Paul hugged her around the waist and walked with
her to the elevator. They waited for one, and when
they got on, two other couples joined them. Belle
mentally sighed with relief. Then as they descended,
each couple got off until they were alone. Six more
floors, and she'd be okay.

Paul backed her into a corner. "You really are
drunk. I don't think I've ever seen you this intoxicated.
That Tristan guy must have really gotten to you."

She was hammered, but something told her to lie.
"He didn't do anything wrong. I was enjoying my best
friend's bachelorette party." At least, that's what she
meant to say. What came out was so garbled it was
barely recognizable as English. "Tristan is wonderful."

His hands rested on her waist. "Yeah, but you miss
us, don't you?" He bent forward and pressed his lips to
hers.

Nausea hit her, and she pushed him back. "No. I don't. We're done. You're marrying Laura."

Paul kissed her again. "Yeah, but you and me...we had something special. We were a good team. I want you back. I've even talked to my boss. He's willing to give you a shot."

"No," she said and pushed him again, but he didn't budge. His mouth was on her, and all she wanted to do was get away. "No."

She realized the elevator had come to a stop, and the doors were open. Tristan's blurry face was red, and his fists were balled.

"I was just—" Paul started to say.

Tristan stormed onto the elevator and loomed over Paul. His lips curled into a snarl. "I told you if you ever touched her again, I'd pound you."

Tristan had rescued her again, but she didn't understand it. He hated her, and she didn't know why.

CHAPTER 12

Tristan wanted to kill Paul. When the elevator door opened, he had his mouth on Belle, and it was all he could do to not coldcock him. "I don't know what you think you were doing, but you'd better never do it with Belle again."

Paul raised his hands like he was the victim. "Hey, she came on to me."

"I doubt that. She can barely stand up straight, and I distinctly heard her say no." Belle's arms slipped around Tristan's neck as he picked her up. "You're pathetic."

The slimeball lifted an eyebrow. "And you're Tristan Stone."

He didn't care if Paul knew his name. Maybe it'd put a little fear into him. With Tristan's connections,

Paul's future in marketing would be questionable. "I'm being generous in allowing you to leave unharmed. You should take the opportunity to go." Tristan smashed the up button with his palm and stalked down the hall. "Belle, are you okay?"

She moaned and lifted her head. "Yeah, I think so."

He pulled her keycard out of her pocket, unlocked her door, and took her inside. "I've looked all over this ship for you. Where have you been?"

"I was avoiding you."

"Yeah, I got that." He sat down with her on the bed and cradled her in his arms. "Why are you in pajamas?"

"It's what Laura wanted. She'd always wanted to be comfortable at her bachelorette party, so this was required attire." Belle giggled. "Say that ten times fast."

Her fuzzy pale-blue pajama pants were cute with little fish all over them, and the matching short sleeve shirt had a fish dead center on it. "Runway's latest?"

"Yeah." She sat up and braced her hand on his chest. "I hid in Laura's room. Did you get the money I owed you? I slipped it under your door like you told me."

He'd gotten it and had sworn he'd give it back. "Yeah, but it's okay. I'm giving it back." Or he would when he thought she'd remember it. He'd been set on telling her who he was, but while he'd searched the ship for her his courage had waned.

Belle leaned forward, her eyes locked with his. "Why are you so kissable?" She rubbed her thumb across his lips. "It's not fair. You always smell so good, and then you wink at me."

Tristan could ask her the same thing. The smell of coconut reminded him of her now. The way she smiled brightened his day, and every time he saw her, he wanted to kiss her. Before he could open his mouth, her lips parted and brushed across his.

He shouldn't kiss her back, but she caught him off guard. His hand slid up her back and into her hair as he closed his eyes. Her lips were sweet and soft. The light, feathery kisses became harder and more demanding. She shifted and straddled him, pressing him against the wall.

His brain finally clicked on. He took her arms and gently pushed her back. "I don't think this is a good idea."

She tilted her head. "But I like kissing you."

"And I like kissing you too. I just don't think tonight is a good night." He was a lot of things, but he wasn't going to be that guy.

She sat back with her arms at her side and stared at him. Her expression turned somber as she tilted her head. "You yelled at me today, and I don't know why. You're my friend, and I'm sorry. Whatever I did, I promise I won't ever do it again." Tears pooled in her eyes, spilled over, and cascaded down her cheeks. "Please don't throw me away. Sometimes I'm not good at being a friend, but I promise I'll be better."

A lump formed in his throat as her words wrapped around his heart and squeezed it like a vice. She hadn't done anything wrong. He'd been mental and had taken it out on her. "You didn't do anything wrong. I was a jerk. I got scared and took it out on you."

Belle collapsed against his chest, and every little sob cut him like a knife. "I'm so sorry for hurting you." He put his arms around her and held her. What was left of his heart was being sliced into two. He'd done more than hurt her.

"Paul needed space too," she said and hiccupped. "Then he left me. Just…gone. He said I was a mess, a trash heap he couldn't be associated with, and so he threw me away." She hiccupped again. "I've never told anyone that. I didn't have Laura, and Momma doesn't understand anymore. It was just me."

He doubted she'd remember anything that happened in the morning, but he'd never forget it. He swallowed down the lump and kissed the top of her head. He didn't know what to say. "I'm sorry" fell flat. "I'm still your friend" sounded stupid. He rubbed his hands up and down her back as she slowly stopped crying. "I think I'm falling in love with you, and it terrifies me. I've thought it before, only to find out they were using me. I'm drawn to you, and I think it'd crush me if you turned out to be the same way."

Little snores answered him. She hadn't heard a word he'd said, but he'd heard it. Now that he'd said it aloud, it was like a light bulb had turned on.

That's what had happened. He wasn't just scared of being deceived; he was falling for her. She was a light-house, and he felt at home with her. If she broke his heart, he wasn't sure he'd ever recover.

BELLE PUSHED against the wall and sat up. Her head hurt, and she didn't feel good. The night before was fuzzier than Target bed slippers. It went beyond being a next-morning hangover.

"Hey," Tristan said.

She blinked her eyes open, and it wasn't a wall she'd pushed on. Well, it was a wall; it was just a wall o'chest.

"Where am I?" Talking hurt. Moving hurt. Existing

hurt. At the moment, if the grim reaper showed up, she'd hop-skip to the afterlife with glee.

"Your room. Do you remember anything?" His voice was filled with concern.

Her head pounded. It felt like a Dremel tool was trying to slice through her skull. "Not really, and I think I drooled on you. Sorry."

Tristan's gaze darted over her face, like he was checking to make sure she wasn't going to fall apart. "It's okay. You were pretty out of it last night. I stayed to make sure you were okay."

The previous day, before she drank the bar dry, came flooding back. "You said you needed space." Her stomach rolled, and she took a deep breath to calm it.

One corner of his mouth turned up, and his dimple showed. "I know. It was stupid."

"We talked about this last night, huh?" She searched her brain for anything to hold on to, but it was a complete blank.

He nodded. "Yeah, but you need to know I'm sorry. I hurt you, and there was no excuse for it."

"Can you tell me what I did so I don't do it again?" The ache from the day before returned, and her chest tightened.

"You didn't do anything wrong. I did. It was irrational and stupid." He held her gaze and took her hands in his. "It won't happen again."

But what if it did? Could she handle it? She cared about him. She was falling for him.

The thought was like a slap. Her head thundered, and her mouth was sticky. She had a wedding to go to. She didn't have time to be thinking about all that... craziness. "It's okay."

"No, it wasn't." His voice was thick and low. "I promise it won't happen again." He used his finger and slashed it over his chest. "Scout's honor."

Belle tilted her head and knitted her eyebrows together. "Were you a scout?"

Tristan chuckled. "No, but I wanted to be. Does that count?"

"No, but it's okay." She leaned forward and brushed the back of her hand against his cheek. "I know people have used you, and it has to be scary, thinking it's happening again. I'm sorry if I did something that made you feel that way."

He pulled her to him. "You didn't. It was all on me. Everything's okay. You did nothing wrong."

"Okay, if you're sure." She inhaled and breathed him in. After thinking she'd lost him, she wanted to soak him in. "It feels late. I'm sure Laura is freaking out, thinking I'm not coming."

"Do you remember anything about being in the elevator with Paul last night?" Tristan asked.

She sat up and touched her head. "No. My head hurts, and I don't feel good—Wait. What happened in the elevator?" *Slow on the uptake, girl, slow on the uptake*, her fuzzy brain said.

Tristan's face had turned red, and his lips were pursed. "Paul was escorting you to your room."

Belle quickly sobered. Her heart raced.

"I was looking all over this ship for you. Nothing happened, but not for his lack of trying."

"He didn't…I didn't…"

He shook his head. "No, sweetheart, he didn't. I told him if he ever touched you again, I'd kill him."

"Sweetheart?"

The smile he shot her made her already cotton mouth feel like it was being stripped. "It fits as a nickname. You do have a sweet heart."

Belle didn't know how to process that, other than she liked how it sounded coming from his lips. "I've lost the taste for alcohol for good. It was stupid. Talk about regretting something. I'll never drink again." At the moment, she'd lost the taste for everything. She wrapped her arms around him. "Thank you. What do I do about Laura? She'll never believe me about Paul."

"Are you sure? Maybe she would now."

"I'm positive. She didn't believe me before, and nothing's changed."

"You can't make people believe what they don't want to believe. She's going to have to figure it out on her own." He rubbed her back. "We should probably get showered and dressed so she doesn't have a meltdown though. It *is* her wedding day."

A soft sigh escaped her lips. She didn't want to move. He was comfortable, and she liked being in his arms. They fit, and it felt good to be with someone who cared about her. "Yeah, you're right, but I am really comfortable, even with the splitting headache."

Tristan held her around the waist and stood. "Get a shower. I'll get you something for your head, and we'll go watch your friend get married."

When he set her down, Belle tiptoed and kissed his cheek. "I'll see you in twenty."

"Not fifteen?"

"I'm not moving that fast today." She couldn't move that fast, but she didn't want him worrying or trying to talk her out of attending Laura's wedding.

He chuckled as he walked to the door and stopped. "You're special to me. I just want you to know that." Without another word, he opened the door and left.

She was special to him. If he only knew how mutual the feeling was.

He'd kept Paul from doing whatever. The thought made her shiver and drove her to the shower. Disgusting pig. Laura was marrying him, and there was no way Belle could protect her from the heartache that was coming.

It was her wedding day. Belle would smile and support her friend, but she'd also be there for her when she needed help picking up the pieces.

There was that pattern again. When would she ever learn?

CHAPTER 13

"Oh, you look beautiful," Belle said as she pinned Laura's hair back with a little sparkly clip. "The dress is perfect." It was perfect. A short little white dress with a flowy skirt and spaghetti straps.

Laura smiled wide and looked from side to side. "I love it. It's perfect for a beach wedding."

"It is." Belle's plastered-on smile was beginning to hurt her cheeks. She hated wanting to rush it, but she wanted to be away from Paul.

With a whirl, Laura turned and ran her fingers through Belle's locks, pushing it over her shoulders. "You look beautiful too. I'm glad we found a dress for you yesterday on board the ship." Her head titled. "You look a little pale though."

Belle felt pale, but she'd do whatever it took to get

through the day. "I'm okay." She looked down as she smoothed out the skirt. Her dress was a strapless dark-green organza and satin. The short dress showed off her legs, and being so dark, it made the freckles on her shoulders stand out big time. She wasn't particularly thrilled with that, but it was the only dress that fit well; so she'd gone with it. "I wish my freckles weren't so prominent."

"Guys love freckles. I bet Tristan sees you and his mouth drops open." Laura patted her shoulder and grabbed two small rose-and-baby's-breath bouquets off the table. "Here ya go."

This was it. Her friend was getting married. Why did she have to be marrying such a snake? If Belle thought Laura would believe her, she'd tell her what happened the night before.

Still, she had to try. If Laura didn't believe her, then that would be on her. "Laura, I need to tell you something that happened last night when Paul—"

Laura held up her hand, cutting her off. "No, I know you don't like him, but this is my wedding day. I love him, Belle. Please just be happy for me."

She should just stop, but she couldn't. If Tristan hadn't shown up...A chill ran down her spine. "But this is important."

"No, Belle, I just need you to be happy for me."

Belle sighed. She'd tried. For some reason, Paul had his claws in her, and Laura was hooked. "I guess we should get out there."

"Thanks for letting me borrow Tristan to walk me down the aisle. He's incredibly sweet."

"Yeah, he is. I really like him. He's become a good friend," Belle mused aloud and quickly added, "and an even better boyfriend."

"Right," Laura said, but her voice sounded strange. "Thank you for being my maid of honor. If you and Tristan weren't attending, it'd just be me, Paul, and the minister. Kind of a small, plain wedding for someone who wanted a huge affair."

It was getting hard to shake off how bad she felt. Another deep breath, and she swallowed down the sick feeling in her stomach. She was *never* drinking again. The hardest thing to hit her stomach from now on would be soda.

"Yeah, but it's not about the wedding, remember? It's about you loving him and him loving you. I think if I ever get married, I want something like this. Small, intimate, and easy. Just a few close friends and the man I marry." Images of Tristan floated to mind, and Belle shook her head. "But today isn't about me. It's about you. Are you ready?"

"Yes." Laura took a deep breath and pushed through the little chapel's front doors.

A small arch was set up with white gauzy material that danced in the breeze. Little pale-pink flowers that matched the bouquets were evenly spaced from one side to the other.

Tristan stood at the edge of a white runner and greeted her with his signature sexy smile. He made her happy. Every time she saw him, butterflies swirled in her stomach. Even as bad as she felt, they flitted like they'd had a case of Red Bull. She could deny it if she wanted, but deep down she knew the truth. She was falling for him. Hard.

His smile widened as they approached, and his mouth parted. "You look beautiful, both of you." He snagged Belle around the waist and put his lips to her ear. "And you are breathtaking."

Her entire face reddened, despite the clamminess that covered her. Belle didn't want him to know how bad she felt, so she smiled wide and said, "I've told you I can't afford new headbands."

"I'll spring for a few." He winked and held his arm out for Laura.

Without access to a cold shower, she wondered if her dress would get ruined if she flung herself into the ocean. Before she could come up with a good comeback, the wedding march began to play. Belle took her place, counted to ten, and slowly walked to the front and stood to the side. Tristan and Laura followed. The minister led Paul through the vows, and then it was Laura's turn.

The minister was repeating the process with Laura when she stopped, teary-eyed. "I'm sorry. I can't."

"What?" Paul asked.

"I can't marry you. I deserve better. I thought I could go through it, but I can't." Laura turned and ran to the church.

Paul narrowed his eyes. "You told her I came onto you, didn't you?"

"No, I didn't." At least she could tell him the absolute truth.

Paul turned on Tristan. "Then it was you."

Tristan shook his head. "It wasn't me. I don't know what happened."

He leveled his eyes at Belle. "Everything was fine until this guy showed up. I know why you like him so much. He's so sensitive. I swear, I thought he was going to cry the other day about his poor dead grandma."

Paul was mostly talk. He said things he knew would throw someone off, but something inside of Belle snapped. All his abuses, taunts, leers...everything swarmed like wasps in her chest. But what really angered her was his sneer about Tristan. He cared for her and had been there when she needed someone. Fury swallowed her whole. The sick feeling she had dissipated long enough for her to ball her hand and swing. The sound of her fist popping echoed down the beach.

"Don't say another word about him, you creep. If you were half the man he is, you might be able to reach his shoes."

He stumbled back and held his jaw. "Yeah, well, your friend in there wants you to think it was an accident or that it just happened that we fell in love. We didn't. She pursued me. And the affair didn't start when the competition did, it started right after you introduced us."

Right, like she'd believe him. "Just stop talking. You'd say anything."

Paul took a step toward Belle, and Tristan put his wall of a body between them. "She said go."

Belle spun on her heel and stormed off to find Laura. The creep. He'd have said anything to try to drive another wedge between them.

She shook out her throbbing hand, hoping Paul's face hurt as bad as her hand. The sick feeling from before reared its ugly head again. Laura needed a shoulder, and she knew what it felt like. Belle could make it through the rest of the day, and she'd rest tonight. Soft cries came from the side of the church as she entered.

"Laura?"

"In here," she replied.

Belle stopped at the door and leaned against the frame. The wood felt nice against her skin, cool and smooth. "I'd ask if you're okay, but I think that's a stupid question."

"No, I'm okay. I just..." Tears spilled down her cheek.

"Wanted to believe he loved you." Belle knew that feeling well. Weeks after the betrayal, she'd found herself still trying to cling to the hope that Paul loved her.

Laura nodded. "Yeah, it was stupid. I was stupid. I'm so sorry. I let that jerk tear our friendship apart. I treated you like dirt, and I should have listened to you."

Belle pushed off the frame and went to Laura. Maybe there was a chance their friendship could be healed over time. Trust was harder to earn, but hearing Laura admit to treating her like dirt gave her hope. She'd never done that before.

"No, you wanted someone to love you. That's not

stupid. The perfect guy for you is out there. You just need to be patient and wait."

She sniffled and plucked a tissue from the box on the desk. "What would I do without you?"

"It wasn't me. You did it. I'm proud of you."

Laura stood and enveloped her in a hug. "I will listen to you from now on. I'll never let a guy come between us again. No matter how much sweet talk he gives me."

"I think that's a good idea." Belle leaned back. "Are we going to get some ice cream and get chip-faced?"

She sniffled again and laughed. "That sounds fantastic. He was such a jerk."

"Yeah, he was. And you deserve better." Had she said that aloud? Yeah, she had. Even Laura deserved some happiness. Belle smiled.

"Now, let's find some ice cream." She was so glad Laura had figured it out before she said I do. How much worse would it have been? At least this way, she was free to find someone who did love her and would treat her right.

A thought popped into Belle's head. If Paul hadn't cheated on her, it might have been her getting married. She'd have missed out on Tristan. When he'd dumped her six months ago, she thought the world was ending. Life may not give second chances, but what if the reason for that was so better things could come along?

Bad things weren't worth holding onto. Next time when she got a bag of lemons, she'd make lemonade and try to do it without complaint.

THE LITTLE BAR they'd found on St. Thomas was filled, but there were no blaring lights. She and Tristan sat together as Laura danced in her chair to the music.

"This is so much better than ice cream," Laura said and tapped her drink against Belle's Sprite-filled glass. "But I do want ice cream before we go back to the ship."

Belle forced a laugh. "Uh, I don't know. Ice cream is pretty hard to beat." Her head had begun to hurt again and her stomach churned, but Laura needed this. She could remember needing a friend and not having one.

"I can't believe you punched Paul," Laura said.

Tristan chuckled. "It was a great punch too. She popped him right in the jaw."

"He had it coming." Belle rubbed her still-aching knuckles.

Laura shook her head, like she still couldn't believe

it. "I wish you'd have a drink with me." She'd pleaded with Belle for over an hour to join her.

"Nope. This fish is firmly on dry land. I think I drank enough last night to fulfill my lifetime quota." Belle punctuated the sentence by taking a gulp of her Sprite.

Laura put the straw to her lips and sipped her drink. "Last night was fun."

"I wouldn't know."

Tristan chuckled. "You were incredibly cute in your fish pajamas."

Belle chuckled. "Oh yeah, I did wear those. That I remember. Circa pre-Jim Beam." Her head swam, and she closed her eyes.

"I can't believe you two aren't a couple," Laura said and pursed her lips.

Belle's eyes flew open, and she froze. "What?"

"You told me last night that you two aren't actually dating."

Cripes. If she had, she didn't mean to.

Tristan put his arm across her shoulder. "We had a fight. We *are* a couple. I was an idiot, and she's more forgiving than I deserve."

Should she keep up the charade? Paul wasn't in the picture any longer. Laura was trying to be a better friend, and yet, Belle couldn't bring herself to tell her the truth. "I thought he hated me."

"Why?" Laura asked.

"I don't know," she said and looked up at Tristan. "We were eating, and I asked a question. Next thing I knew, he got angry and left."

Tristan put his lips to her ear and whispered, "I have been to San Juan before. It was an innocent question that should've been given a simple answer."

His breath tickled her neck, and a giggle popped out. Without thinking, she leaned into him. "And that was all?"

"That was all."

"I feel like a third wheel here." Laura put her drink down. "I want to dance. You guys want to dance?"

Belle shook her head. "Uh, I think we established in high school that I don't dance." There was no way she was going to dance, even if she could. Her stomach churned like a riptide now. One step, and she'd be on the floor.

"What happened?" asked Tristan.

Laura burst out laughing. "She's horrible. It's like pool with music."

"Exactly. It's like pool, only," Belle waved a hand over her body, "this is the weapon of choice."

Tristan threw his head back and laughed. "It's that bad?"

She loved his warm laugh. "It's that bad."

"Wow, then no dancing for you." He kissed her cheek. "If there's a slow dance, you can stand on my feet, okay? I won't let you hurt anyone."

"Okay." If she could just make it a little longer, she'd be in the clear.

Tristan looked at her and kissed her forehead. "Are you feeling okay? You feel a little warm."

"I'm fine. With all these bodies, it's hot in here to me."

"It *is* hot." Laura stood. "Since you dance, you can dance the fast dances with me."

"I appreciate the offer, but I'm not really a fast dancer. Honestly, I'm not really into clubs. I like quiet places." Tristan drained the rest of his water. "I don't want to dance."

She turned her big doe eyes on him and stuck her bottom lip out. "Please."

Tristan rolled his eyes. "Does that usually work?"

Belle nodded. "Yeah, it usually does. Over the years, she's perfected it."

"Sorry. Doesn't work on me." Tristan shrugged and mumbled, "I've seen it all."

How many times had Tristan rescued Belle? She

was glad for the chance to do the same for him. "Laura, he doesn't want to dance. I kinda like him near me. I don't really want him to leave."

Laura chewed her lip. "Just one? Just to shake this funk off of me? I thought I was marrying the love of my life today."

Tristan tucked a piece of Belle's hair behind her ear. "Okay, just one."

Belle needed to bail him out. "I'll dance with you, Laura." She hoped she could stand long enough to satisfy Laura.

"You will?" Laura smiled.

He shook his head. "No, I can do it."

"She's my friend. I'll do it."

Tristan stood. "I've got this. One fast song, and I'll be right back." He leaned down and kissed the top of her head. "I'll be the tall guy looking completely out of place."

"Are you sure?"

"Yeah," he said and winked.

Laura bounced over to Tristan, grabbed his hand, and began pulling him to the dance floor. "Oh, thank you so much!"

He was so cute. In five days, he'd invaded her world, and she was having trouble seeing a world without him. She was falling head over heels for him. There was nothing fuzzy in her head about that.

Her eyes went wide, and then she squeezed them shut. A picture floated through her head. She was the one ring, he was Frodo, and she was being thrown into the king of all dooms, Mt. Doom. What was she going to do? She couldn't fall for him.

Anytime something in her life was too good to be true, it usually was. Who knew what Murphy had in mind for her with as great as he seemed. She needed to cool her jets before she got seriously whammied. Her stomach flipped, and she pressed her forehead on the table top. The frosty tile felt amazing.

She swallowed down the sour taste creeping up her throat and straightened. All the bodies moving and the heat…all she wanted was for everything to stop. There was no more hiding how bad she felt. Crossing her arms on the table, she laid her head down and closed her eyes. If she could be still a while, she'd be fine. Maybe.

CHAPTER 14

Tristan looked over his shoulder as Laura pulled him to the dance floor, and his eyebrows drew together. "Laura, I don't think Belle feels good."

"What? She's fine. Let's dance." Laura stopped and started rocking side to side.

He pointed in Belle's direction. "That doesn't look fine to me. I really think she's sick. She's been pale all day, and she hasn't eaten anything that I can recall. I thought she was just upset about decking Paul, but I think it's more than that."

She waved him off and continued to dance. "No, she's fine. She's probably still tired from last night. I mean, she was wanting to dance just a second ago."

He stood stone-still and crossed his arms over his chest, just looking at her.

Laura stopped dancing. "What?"

"I'm trying to decide if you're just that unaware or if you're just that selfish. Your so-called best friend is sick, and you're so wrapped up in you, you aren't willing to even investigate."

She huffed. "Belle is fine. She's always fine. And it is about me. I was supposed to be getting married today. She's supposed to be cheering me up, and there she is, sitting at the table being a downer."

This woman was crazy, selfish, or both. Maybe she'd had too much to drink. Surely, she couldn't be this ambivalent towards someone she cared about.

"You do whatever you want. I'm going to check on her," Tristan said and returned the table. He touched Belle's shoulder, and she lifted her head. "You don't feel good, do you?"

Belle shook her head. "I'm sorry. I thought I could keep it together a little longer, but I feel so bad. Laura's going to be upset with me."

Tristan looked in the direction he'd left Laura. "I'm sure she'll understand."

"No, you go ahead and dance with her. I'll just…"

She slid off the stool, and Tristan caught her as she staggered.

"I'll go to my room." She went slack in his arms, her eyes glazed over. "I'll be fine."

He took her face in his hand and then touched her forehead. She was blazing hot. "You're not fine."

"Oh, great, more drama from her," Laura said as she stopped at the table and wobbled a bit. Maybe that was it. Maybe she was just a nasty drunk.

Tristan glared at her. "What?" How was Belle friends with this woman?

"It was supposed to be my wedding day, so, of course, she'd have to make it about her." Laura rolled her eyes and crossed her arms over her chest. "She does it all the time."

He was done with Laura. "I'm taking Belle to the ship's doctor. You can come or not. I really don't care."

"Fine." Laura yanked her bag off the back of the chair. "Let's go."

TRISTAN STOOD next to Belle as the doctor examined her. Little beads of sweat lined her forehead, and she was so pale her lips looked white. "Is it food poisoning?"

"Could be. Or it could be she overexerted herself. She was out late, up early, and part of a wedding."

Doctor Horowitz looked at the clipboard he was holding.

Laura grunted. "My wedding didn't actually happen. I got to the vows and decided I could do better."

Tristan glanced at her. Unbelievable. He wasn't impressed with her to start with, and now he liked her even less. He hadn't liked how she'd pushed herself on Belle, even when Belle seemed to be begging for a little space. She was just awful.

"I'll never drink again," Belle moaned.

Laura giggled. "Yeah, she was up late last night. She had a little too much to drink too."

"And then there's that. It could just be a bad hangover." Dr. Horowitz looked at her sympathetically. He dropped his hands to his side and let the clipboard dangle at his fingertips. "You can take her to her room and keep pushing fluids. I think someone should stay with her too."

Belle groaned, turned on her side, and curled into a ball facing him. "No, I'll be fine," she mumbled without opening her eyes. "I just need sleep."

Tristan looked at Laura.

"She'd probably be more comfortable if I stayed with her," Laura said.

He scoffed. "I don't think so."

"I didn't realize how sick she was. Now that I know, I'll take care of her."

Tristan didn't like it.

Belle touched his hand and mumbled, "It's okay."

He pushed her hair back from her face. Leaving her with Laura didn't sit well with him. "I'll stay with you."

Belle gave him a weak smile, but her eyes remained closed. Her hand covered his, and all he wanted to do was pick her up and shield her from everything. Tristan leaned down and touched his lips to her cheek.

Laura let out an exaggerated sigh. "I'll take care of her."

"Fine."

When the doctor released Belle, Tristan carried her to her room. He laid her on the bed and covered her up. "If you need anything, I'll be next door, okay?"

She nodded and rolled to her side. He wasn't ready to leave. He couldn't shake the feeling that leaving her with Laura was wrong. She'd proven she was selfish and didn't have Belle's best interest in mind. What if she didn't pay attention and Belle got dehydrated again? He looked at Laura as he stood. "Promise me, if she needs something, please come get me."

Laura tugged at the pendant hanging on the gold chain around her neck. "I will. She'll be fine. You don't have to worry."

The corner of her mouth quirked up, and she saun-tered up to him. "You two really aren't dating, are you?"

"*Yes*, we are." Maybe what Paul said about her wasn't so far off. "I care about her."

She lifted one eyebrow. "Right."

He was going to set her straight now, because if Belle wasn't in the picture, he still wouldn't be inter-ested in Laura. She was no different than the other women he'd dated. "I'm with Belle. She's amazing, and I care about her. I'm sure, being her best friend, that you aren't interested in me anyway, right?"

"Oh, no, I was just…curious." She smiled.

Tristan took one last look at Belle and left the room. He needed to get out before he said something really nasty to Laura. Maybe he could find a way to warn her about the way Laura had been acting. She wasn't a good friend, but Belle might need to come to that conclusion on her own. Hopefully, it would be before Laura hurt her again.

It made him wonder if Laura had hurt her before. He would ask when she felt better, and he hoped he was wrong about her so-called friend. For Belle's sake.

~

BELLE STRETCHED long and wiped her mouth. The sun was peeking through the small window in her room. She sat up and looked around. How had she gotten to her room? When had she gotten to her room? She looked down at her arm. And why did she have a bandage on? What time was it? All the questions pinged like they were a rubber ball bouncing off a wall.

"It's almost lunchtime, and you've missed some of your time to visit Amber Cove," Laura said as she leaned against the door to the bathroom. "You were sick last night. Why didn't you say anything?"

Wow, the next day? It hadn't been that late when they went to the club. She must have been feeling pretty bad to sleep that long. "It was your wedding day. You dumped Paul. I didn't want to make a fuss."

"You could have told me. Once I ditched Paul, we could have come back here, and you could have rested." She pushed off the frame to cross the room and sit beside Belle. "Friends should be able to tell each other everything."

Belle nodded. They should be, but something inside Belle was keeping her from being honest with Laura. She'd forgiven her, but the broken trust wasn't something that could be easily repaired. "I know. I wasn't keeping it from you. I thought I could handle it until we got back on board."

"Obviously, that wasn't the case. Next time say something. We're friends. We're supposed to take care of each other." Laura took Belle's hands in hers. "And that means I need to be honest with you."

What did that mean? Alarm bells sounded as Belle looked at Laura. "Okay." She had a feeling whatever was about to come out of Laura's mouth was going to be far from the truth.

"Tristan hit on me." Her eyebrows formed a "w" as she looked at Belle. "I'm really sorry. I guess we know how to pick 'em, huh?"

She was definitely lying. Tristan wouldn't have hit on her, and Belle knew that as well as she knew anything. Why would Laura be lying about him? "He did?"

Her head bobbed up and down. "Yeah, he did. When we got you back to your room, he made a pass at me. Tried to kiss me. I told him no and that we were friends. I've learned my lesson. I'll never do that again."

Belle pulled her hands from Laura's. "Right."

"You believe me, don't you? I promised if it ever happened again, I'd tell you right away. I don't want what happened with Paul to ever happen again." Those doe eyes were trained on Belle like missiles.

"No, I don't either." How was she supposed to handle this? Should she just tell Laura she flat out didn't believe her, or did she let it slide? Was what Paul said true? He was a liar and a cheat. A downright snake in the grass.

Was she reading too much into it? Could Laura have misread something Tristan said? She couldn't picture him trying to kiss Laura. Something was smelling, and Denmark was calling.

"Are you going to tell him to take a hike?" She smiled sympathetically.

No, but she might once again consider pushing Laura overboard. "Not yet. I want to confront him first."

"Oh, please let me be there. I bet he thought he could get away with it." She wiggled like it was just a joke.

She'd accused Tristan of coming on to her. That wasn't funny, and Belle didn't take it lightly. Tristan was a good man. What would Laura gain by lying about him?

"Uh, no, I'd like to do that on my own."

"Okay," she said and pouted. "I guess I can understand that."

Belle threw the covers off. She was hungry, still a little tired, and, more than anything, she wanted to see Tristan. "I'm going to get a shower. I'm starved."

"I'm hungry too, so that sounds good." Laura stood and helped Belle up. "I'll be ready and waiting when you're ready to go. Maybe we could make it a girl's thing. That way you don't have to deal with Tristan today."

"We'll see. He has a knack for showing up. Let me get my shower. I'll be right back." She went to the bathroom without waiting for a response.

In the bathroom, Belle pushed down the feeling of dread pooling in her stomach. How many times had Laura told her that one of Belle's boyfriends had come on to her? How many times did Laura like the same guys she did? More frequently than Belle cared to remember. Everything was always about Laura, and when it wasn't, she did something so that it *was* about her.

In high school, they hung out when it was convenient...for Laura. Like when she thought she was going to fail something, or when she was between boyfriends and had nothing better to do. Belle was the friend version of a consolation prize. How had she not seen that before now? Why didn't she figure it out sooner? And why didn't that epiphany hurt worse?

Maybe her friendship with Laura needed a little more soul-searching than she thought. She'd forgiven her, and she still forgave her. That didn't mean she trusted her or that the relationship didn't need a high-powered magnifying glass and some introspection. Yeah, something didn't smell right. Why had it taken her this long to wise up? She hoped by the time her shower was over, she'd have an answer.

CHAPTER 15

*L*unch was bland, boring, and slow. Belle set her
elbow on the table and put her head in her
hand as she pushed her food around with her
fork. She didn't want to be alone with Laura. What she
wouldn't give to see Tristan. Listening to Laura was
giving her another headache. If she thought it'd work,
she'd feign being sick again and retreat to her room,
but Laura would just follow her, especially now that
she was bunking with Belle—unfortunately— after
breaking things off with Paul.

"You look so bummed. I'm thinking I shouldn't
have told you. I should have just kept it to myself and
made sure we were never alone again," Laura said,
finishing the last few bites on her plate.

Belle straightened. "I'm fine. I think I'm still getting over whatever it was I had."

"Hey," Tristan said, his deep voice coming from behind her.

She turned and smiled. If Laura wasn't there, she'd have thrown her arms around him, hugged him, and smothered him in kisses. On second thought, it was probably a good thing she wasn't alone. No matter how much she liked his company, they were still just friends. "Hi."

"Laura." His tone wasn't harsh, but it wasn't friendly either.

"Tristan." She mimicked his tone. "It's a girls-*only* lunch. We'll see you later."

Belle leveled her eyes at Laura. "No, we won't. I like Tristan, and he's staying."

Her skin tingled as he took her face in his hands, making Laura's presence more like a gnat in a windstorm. "I wanted to make sure you feel better."

Belle studied his face. No, he was different. She felt that all the way to her soul. It was bone deep and profound. He was special. She was positive Tristan hadn't come on to Laura.

She shrugged. "I'm okay." Physically, she was okay. The rest of what she felt was a mix that she couldn't put her finger on.

He shot her a half-smile. It was still her favorite sexy, sweet smile. He gently pressed his lips to hers. They lingered there, full of promise, before he slowly pulled back. "Strawberries?"

Her cheeks heated. "Yeah."

With one more kiss, he let her face go. "Good choice." He winked, and her cheeks burned even more.

She tangled her fingers in his. "When we're done with lunch, we're going to mill around Amber Cove. You want to come?"

"Belle." Laura's tone was sharp. "We're doing a girls day, not just lunch."

"Yeah, and we're two women going out on our own in a strange town. I don't think it'd hurt to have a hulking guy walking with us to ward off any potential problems." She wanted Tristan along. If Laura didn't want to hang out with him, fine, but that didn't mean Belle had to ditch him. And she wouldn't. If she had to pick, she'd pick Tristan.

Laura huffed and crossed her arms over her chest. "I guess so."

Even if Tristan had come on to Laura, Belle wasn't ready to give him up. It's not like Laura hadn't known the truth about Paul. How long did she continue her relationship with him? She could stick a sock in it.

Tristan ran his fingertips across her cheek and cupped her chin. "You sure you feel okay?"

"I'm okay." She didn't want to tell him she had a lot on her mind. That Paul was telling the truth, and that her friend was trying to come between them. Although, there really wasn't a "them."

"I'll grab something for lunch that I can take with me. We don't have long before we have to be back. We could go walking on the beach, look around in the shops...I'm good with whatever."

Why did the world cease to exist when he was around? What was it about him that drowned out every bad thing and made her feel like the only person in the room?

"Let's go zip-lining," Laura said.

Tristan pulled his gaze from hers and leveled his eyes at Laura. "She was so sick she nearly passed out last night. I don't think zip-lining is a good idea."

"Belle's fine. We're in the Dominican Republic. We should do something more fun than swimming or shopping." The way Laura looked at Tristan made Belle want to deck her too. "And she's a grown woman. She can do what she wants. *Right*, Belle?" Her look was the kind she got when Laura wanted her to take a side: hers.

She was about to be disappointed. Tristan was

right. She didn't feel like zip-lining. It sounded fun, and she'd wanted to do that. But she was also tired, and venturing out was about all she could handle. "I don't want to zip-line. I'm still a little tired, and I think relaxing on the beach sounds like a great day."

Tristan's attention landed on her again, and she could feel him giving her some of his strength. "You don't have to anything you don't want to do."

Laura glowered at Tristan and whined, "Come on. It's not like we're here every day. You can push through and handle it."

Silently, Belle prayed she wouldn't make a scene in the dining hall. "No. If you want to go, I'll go with you and wait for you at the bottom. I'm not up to it, and I can't push through it."

Tristan stepped next to Belle and put his arm across her shoulder. "She said no. You need to listen to her."

With a huff, Laura stood. "I thought you were ditching him. You said you believed me. I guess that was just a lie. I should have known you'd pick his side. Turnabout's fair play, right?"

Belle didn't have the energy or patience for one of Laura's temper tantrums. She glared at Laura. "I guess you're right. I mean, I did tell you about Paul, and you stuck with him for how many months after? You almost married him, knowing he'd ruined my career and I had proof. So, forgive me if I don't jump at the chance to break things off with Tristan."

Her lower lip trembled. "You're right. I did. I'm sorry. I just don't want a repeat of last time."

"There won't be." Belle's tone was confident. Tristan wasn't Paul. He was a good man, and she knew it. "And I'm not zip-lining. It's not because of Tristan; it's because I don't want to. I'm not going to do it."

"Okay, I just didn't want you to regret not doing it while you were here." She took her seat again. "And Tristan, I forgive you. Just don't let it happen again."

Tristan's eyebrows knitted together. "Let what happen again?"

"You know what you did. Don't play. Just do what I said, and don't let it happen again." Laura stared him down.

Belle discreetly took his hand and squeezed it. "He won't." She stood, tiptoed, and quickly whispered, "Just go along with it, and we'll talk later."

He locked eyes with Laura. "Okay, whatever you say, Laura." He put his arm around Belle's waist and then held her gaze. "I'm looking forward to spending some time with you today."

She grinned. "Then get something to eat so we can go."

He let go of her and winked as he walked toward the buffet line. Belle sat again and took a few bites of her food while Laura droned on about Tristan and his nerve. She didn't care one whit what she had to say about him. He was her friend, and she was falling for him. Laura would just have to suck it up.

Or she could just leave. Belle would need time to decide which sounded better. Although, leaving sounded great.

"You're going to make me fall asleep," Tristan said as Belle combed her fingers through his hair. His head was in her lap as they lounged on a blanket at the ocean's edge. The water would rush to shore, but they were far enough away that it didn't splash. It was just a gentle touch by the time it reached them. She stopped and held his face. He opened his eyes, and she was just staring at him. "What?"

"I'm glad I met you." There was something in her tone that almost felt wistful.

"Are you sure? That first time we met, you didn't seem all that happy." He chuckled.

Her smile didn't quite reach her eyes. "The first

thing Paul ever said to me was that I had pretty eyes. It was a scary ghost."

He had plenty of those, so he could understand that. "I'm sorry."

"It's okay. You didn't know. You were giving me a compliment." She started combing her fingers through his hair again.

She had a habit of excusing people's behavior, whether it was warranted or not. He wondered if she realized it, but he didn't want to cause tension when it'd been such a nice day. Then it hit him that tomorrow they'd be back at sea, headed home, and he had one last thing to do for his grandmother.

"What's wrong?" she asked.

His eyes snapped open. "What?"

"You sighed like your heart was broken." It felt like she was staring right through him.

Tristan was so glad Laura went zip-lining. Not having her around had made everything more relaxed, and he didn't have to watch himself so closely. "My grandmother wanted me to spread her ashes on the voyage back to Miami. I've pushed it out of my mind until now, and I can't any longer because that's tomorrow."

Belle caressed his cheek with her fingertips. "I can't imagine how that feels. I'm sorry you're hurting."

He was missing her, but he wasn't hurting like he was when he started the trip. The loneliness he'd felt when he booked the trip seemed a million light years away. In the last seven days, he'd felt happier than he had in years.

"Actually, I'm doing okay. I'm sad she's gone, but I'm okay." If he let himself dig a little deeper, he'd find a name associated with his newfound happiness. He quickly put the shovel down and backed away from the hole. That was *not* something he needed to be doing.

She was staring at him again, smiling.

"What?" he asked through a chuckle.

"Nothing. I'm just listening."

He sat up and spun in the sand to face her. "Just listening, huh?"

"Yeah, you were talking, so I was listening." A small breeze picked up and tossed her hair across her face, and her dark-green eyes peeked through. It was something out of a photo shoot, and it felt like the wind was whispering in his ear to kiss her.

He scooted closer and pushed her hair out of her face. "You're one of only a few people to say that to me, and I believe it."

"Your grandmother took you in when you were ten. She raised you, loved you, and taught you how to be a gentleman. You cared for her when she was sick, and now you miss her. Spreading her ashes is like saying the final goodbye. I would be sad too." She held his gaze as she said it. "I listen because you have something to say, and sometimes you're not using words. I listen because...I don't want to miss what you're not saying."

Either the sand was getting in his eyes, or he was actually tearing up. If he spoke, he wasn't sure he could finish. He wasn't sure he had words to begin with, and the lump in his throat was making it hard to breathe.

How on earth did someone like him meet someone like her? If he hadn't taken the cruise, would he have ever met her? Why weren't the women in his world like this? Did money make people lose their humanity over time? Had he lost his? He didn't feel that he had, but spending time with Belle made him question things he'd never had reason to question before.

Her arms circled his neck, and she kissed his cheek. "I didn't mean to upset you."

He wrapped his arms around her and tried not to hold on as tightly as he wanted. "You didn't. I just didn't know what to say." He didn't want to be alone when he said goodbye to his grandmother, either. "Would you...would you stay with me while I spread her ashes?" It was weird to be asking her. His head was not where it was supposed to be.

"I wouldn't miss it." Her voice was soft, and she squeezed him as she said it.

"Thank you." He inhaled and breathed her in, coconut and salt air.

She pulled back. "It's going to be okay."

"I know." He quickly looked around and then locked gazes with her. He was quiet a moment and then asked, "Laura told you I came on to her, didn't she?"

"Yes."

Tristan cursed under his breath. "Do you believe her?"

"No."

"Why?"

Belle smiled. "Because you aren't that guy."

"Why do you trust me? She's your friend." He earnestly wanted an answer to that question. What had he done to deserve her trust?

"I don't know if she was ever really my friend. But you are, and I just do." She shrugged.

Man, he wanted to kiss her. He shouldn't. He shouldn't want to. "I really want to kiss you." He needed to remember that rubber band idea.

"Probably shouldn't. I don't think friends kiss." She smiled.

When he leaned closer, her smile vanished. His heart was beating a million times a minute. "I don't think so either." Yeah, he was going to kiss her. It was probably a huge mistake. And at that moment, he just didn't care.

He brushed his lips across her cheek, and she immediately tangled her fingers in his hair.

"I'm sorry," he whispered.

"Me too," she said breathlessly and pressed her lips to his.

No, he wasn't sorry. Not at all. He put his arm around her waist and drew her onto his lap. With every touch of her lips, he became dizzier. He loved the feel of her against him. Her skin was soft, and her touch was gentle.

He braced his hand on the blanket as he eased her back onto it. She wrapped one of her legs around his and untangled one hand from his hair. Her fingertips slowly trailed down his back in a feathery touch that left goosebumps in their wake.

Like an invitation, her lips parted with a soft moan, and he accepted, deepening the kiss. He curled his body around her, letting the world fall away as he let the feel of her sink into him. All that was left was the two of them and the sound of the waves hitting the shore.

If time could freeze, he'd do it. She was all he wanted.

"Ahem." Laura's voice froze things all right, just not time.

He groaned.

"I take it you two didn't miss me." Her tone was snipped and catty.

The corners of Belle's lips quirked up as she looked into Tristan's eyes. "Not particularly, no."

"What is wrong with you? You weren't like this before you met him." Laura's tone was as petulant as she was.

Belle didn't take her eyes off of him. "Laura, I'm on an exotic beach with the most beautiful man I've ever laid eyes on. He's kind, caring, sweet, and he saved my life. And not only do I like him, but to top off all that greatness, he was kissing me. If roles were reversed, would you have missed me?" Belle pulled her gaze from his and they both looked up at Laura, whose arms were crossed over her chest.

"Okay, I'll give you that." He'd really expected her to say something else. Something snottier.

With Laura's return, their sorry-not-sorry make out session was over. Laura didn't want to swim or stay in one place, so the three of them wandered around Amber Cove until it was time to return to the ship.

Laura was a spoiled brat that only someone like Belle would put up with. Belle had been kidding when she first said she wanted to throw her overboard. Now he was thinking she may have been onto something.

CHAPTER 16

When the elevator doors opened,
Ashley, Maritsa, and Shawn greeted
Tristan, Belle, and Laura, who was tagging along
everywhere now that Paul was out of the picture.

"Hey, guys, we're gathering in the game lounge,
and it's required attendance," Ashley said.

Belle looked up at Tristan. "Oh, well, required
attendance. We'd better go." She smiled. "I need to
change though. I feel sticky from the day."

He loved her humor. "Me too."

Laura cleared her throat. "I'm her best friend,
Laura."

"Yeah, we met these guys the first day we were
here. They're also cruise winners," Belle said.

Maritsa, Shawn, and Ashley each shook hands with Laura.

"It's nice to meet you." Laura said. "Game lounge? Can I come? I can actually play pool without the fear of death." She laughed, but Tristan noticed Belle didn't laugh with her. Instead, she looked at the ground. How long had Laura used her to make herself look good?

"Yes, but what she lacks in pool skills she more than makes up in kindness and beauty. Anyone can learn to play pool. What she's got can't be taught." He winked when she looked up at him.

Belle looked down again as a rosy blush tinted her cheeks.

His Aunt Felicia appeared behind Ashley, and his heart sank. She was going to out him. "Ms. Evans, we need to talk."

Not him. Belle was in trouble. Paul Whitlock. That jerk had complained.

Belle looked up, and her eyes went wide. She'd had the same thought. "Oh, no. Oh, I'm so stupid." She smacked her forehead. "Why did I let him bait me?"

Maritsa's eyebrows knitted together as she looked at Belle. "What happened?"

"I'll tell you later," she whispered and started to follow Felicia.

He followed too. There was no way he was letting her go alone.

His aunt stopped and turned. "Mr. Davis, your presence isn't required."

"Is this about Paul Whitlock? If so, I was a witness to what happened," Tristan said.

Felicia tipped her chin in Laura's direction. "Did you witness it too?"

"Oh, no."

"Then I just need you two, Ms. Evans, Mr. Davis." Her dark-brown eyebrow went up. She held his gaze a moment. "Come this way, please."

They walked in silence until they reached the office. His aunt shut the door and took a seat behind her desk. "You punched another passenger. You broke the rules. You do realize you're going to have to pay back everything, correct? The cruise and the cash."

The color drained from Belle's face. "No, please. What can I do to fix this?"

Aunt Felicia sat back in her chair and crossed her arms over her chest. "Ms. Evans, there is no fixing this. Mr. Whitlock has threatened to sue the cruise line if we don't take action."

"But I can't return the cash or pay it back. Please. I'll apologize. I'll do it publicly. Whatever he wants... but please don't make me pay it back. If that happens, my mom can't stay in the nursing home. She needs it. If I take her out, I may not be able to get her back in." Panic filled her voice. "Please."

Her mom was in the nursing home? Oh, man. "There are extenuating circumstances here."

His aunt lifted an eyebrow. "Mr. Davis, we'll talk after I've finished with Ms. Evans."

"Please, Ms. Fredericks, please." Belle's bottom lip trembled, and she sat down in one of the two chairs facing the desk. "I'll do anything Mr. Whitlock wants me to do. Anything at all."

"He wants you punished."

Belle's shoulders rounded, and she hung her head. "Okay. I understand. Life doesn't give you second chances. I did it. I'm sorry." She stood. "I'll have to work out a payment arrangement. I don't have it on hand. The only reason I was able to go on this cruise at all was because I was able to use the cash to pay the nursing home and get ahead."

"For now, we'll just say the verdict's pending until I finish with Mr. Davis. I do need to talk to him alone, so that'll be all."

She nodded, but he could tell she wasn't there. "Yes, ma'am." Without looking at him, she left the office.

"You're not really going to make her pay it back, are you?" Tristan asked.

His aunt stood, walked around the desk, and pulled him into a hug. "Darling, it is so good to see you. What are you doing on this ship as a passenger in an interior room and not a grand suite?"

He shrugged. "I wanted to be anonymous, and Grandmother wanted me to take a cruise on this ship and spread her ashes on the voyage home."

"You're lucky I'm quick-witted. I could have outed you that day." She pulled back and pinched his cheek. "You look great, love."

His aunt was twenty years younger than his grand-mother in age, and forty years younger in attitude. Her slim figure, smooth face, and current hairstyle made her look like she was in her forties. "You do too."

"So, tell me about her. I can see you're smitten. She's a cute little thing." They sat at the same time, and his aunt smiled like she knew something he didn't.

He should have known she'd see it. "She has no idea who I am. She's sweet to a fault. Kind. She punched that Whitlock guy because he was making fun of me. And, if you'll check the video footage from the elevator last night, you'll see him groping her while she was drunk."

Her lips curled. "Disgusting pig. I'll check the video feed." He loved that she never questioned him. If he said it, she believed him. Probably helped that he'd also never lied to her.

"He is. He dumped her and had an affair with her best friend." His mouth felt nasty just saying it.

"Poor thing. Did you know her mother is in a nursing home? She doesn't look old enough for that." She crossed her legs and sat back.

He shook his head. "No, I had no idea, and any time it's brought up, she changes the subject."

"She was breaking my heart. The look on her face. The girl was beside herself. And then the second chance thing? What has she been through to have such an outlook like that?"

Tristan shook his head and shrugged. "I don't know, but she has her masters in marketing."

"What?" She sat forward. "On her release forms where it asked about that, all she wrote was that she works two jobs. One as an administrative assistant, and another as a waitress in some little diner I've never heard of."

Two jobs? "They worked together and competed for the same account. Paul sabotaged her presentation and her career." And yet, she was still kind and trusting.

His aunt lifted an eyebrow. "Sounds like we need to

find out what firm he's with and make sure we avoid it."

"Believe me, I'm going to make sure that happens." Tristan chuckled. He loved his aunt. She was a lot like his grandmother in the way she saw the world, and the two of them were eye to eye on business most of the time.

"Oh, love, how are you doing? I mean the real answer, not the one you give people in passing." She covered his hand with hers. "I miss her."

He wasn't missing her as much in the last seven days. "I'm doing okay. I miss her still."

"But Belle Evans has a needle and thread, mending that heart of yours, huh?" She smiled.

Tristan rubbed his palms down his jeans. "We're just friends. She doesn't want to be in a relationship, and I'm here to fulfill Grandma's wishes. I don't need any complications."

"Is your heart on board with that, or is it going rogue?" She snickered.

He rolled his eyes. "Stop it, Aunt Felicia. She is just a friend. It's going to stay that way." If he weren't sitting with his aunt, he'd have burst out laughing at himself. He was falling for her. Had been falling for her. He couldn't stop wanting to kiss her. He needed a straightjacket.

"Oh, I'm sure that's absolutely true." The deadpan look she gave him was classic Aunt Felicia.

"I'm serious."

"I am too." She lifted her head an inch and looked down her nose at him. "See, I can play the game as well as anyone else."

Tristan exhaled sharply. "I can't get involved with her. We're from completely different worlds. She would hate everything about my world. I couldn't do that to her."

His aunt uncrossed her legs, leaned forward, and touched his knee. "Honey, the way that girl was looking at you, she'd live on Mars if it meant she got to be with you."

"No, we're just friends. She doesn't want to be in a relationship, and…neither do I." He couldn't let himself think that way. Belle didn't want a relationship.

"Darling, you can lie to yourself, but not to me."

He jumped out of the chair and raked a hand through his hair. "We have a friendship, and I like it. I don't want to mess it up by making it complicated and confusing. I enjoy spending time with her, and she's not ready to be in a relationship. I don't care how you think she was looking at me."

His aunt stood and held his face. "Calm down, love.

If neither of you are ready, then neither of you are ready. I'm just an old woman."

"You are not an old woman. You told me at your last birthday you'd just turned twenty-five." He winked.

She pinched his cheek. "You were always my favorite nephew."

"Only because I'm the only one."

"Don't sell yourself short. Who says that wouldn't be true if you had competition?"

He hugged her and lifted her off the ground. "I love you. If I didn't have you, life would be boring."

"Oh, darling, truer words have never been spoken. Now, put me down. That's not dignified." She snorted.

Tristan threw his head back and laughed. Leave it to her to make him laugh. "Neither is snorting like a pig."

"Don't discount pigs. Bacon is delicious."

He grew serious. "Do you want to be with me when I spread her ashes?" He'd asked Belle, but Felicia was his grandmother's daughter. It was only right to ask her.

"Oh, honey, no. We said our goodbyes. You two were as thick as thieves. My mother loved you like you were her baby. There was never a time I spoke to her that your name wasn't mentioned. You were the light of her life. She was so proud of you and the man you are. I think you need this last goodbye." She smiled and patted his cheek.

"Okay." His grandmother was proud of him. She'd said so, but hearing it from someone else made him happy. "Were you ever jealous?" He didn't know why that popped into his head.

Aunt Felicia laughed. "Oh, darling, no. Mother and I had a fabulous relationship. I didn't have anything to be jealous of. I lost my brother, and it devastated me. I can't imagine what it must have been like for you. No, I was never jealous. I had all the love I needed."

They sat back down and talked well into the night. He hadn't realized how much he'd missed her. If nothing else, if—and it was a big if—somehow something happened with Belle, his aunt would welcome her with open arms.

CHAPTER 17

Tristan yawned as he shuffled to his room after leaving his aunt's office. He shouldn't have stayed up so late, but he couldn't miss the opportunity to spend time with her away from board meetings, fancy dinners, and stupid attendance-required fundraisers.

They'd gotten so caught up in their conversation, he'd forgotten Belle was still thinking she was going to have to pay the money back. He should've kept better track of the time. He hadn't meant to let her worry. First thing tomorrow, he'd give her the good news that she was off the hook.

He stopped a few doors away. With her shoulder leaned against his door, Laura held an empty ice bucket. "Late night date?"

How did she know to be by his door this late? "No, just speaking with the passenger liaison for the cruise winners, explaining what happened with Paul. Since, you know, I was a witness."

She pushed off the door, set the bucket on the floor, and slowly walked toward him. "Have any plans for the rest of the night?"

Other than avoiding her? Nope. "I have plans to get a good night's sleep. Alone. In my own room."

She stopped a few feet away. "You sure?"

He studied her, and his curiosity got the better of him. "Does Belle know you're like this? I mean, she said you've known each other a long time. Since high school, right? How have you been friends for so long, behaving like this?"

"She makes excuses for me. I'm desperate to be loved, so I'm easy for guys to manipulate. I'm oblivious, so I don't realize I'm hurting her. I mean, you've seen her do it. She does it for everyone. She's the very definition of a doormat. Someone like me needs someone like her to find the good ones." She took a step. "Which is why I let Paul go. She'd found someone better."

Tristan was stunned. All this time, he thought she was just being selfish and self-centered, but not on purpose. He just thought she was unware of it, or he hoped she was, for Belle's sake. A response was on the tip of his tongue, but for the life of him, he couldn't get it out.

"I know who you are, by the way." She was trying to be sultry or sexy or something, but it was just coming across as desperate. Not desperate for love, just desperate in general.

"I really don't want to know the answer to that, but I do have a few questions," Belle said, and they both startled.

Laura plastered on a quick smile as she walked back and snatched up the bucket. "Oh, Belle, you're up. I was just going to get the ice."

"Is that before or after you tried to seduce my boyfriend? I mean, you did promise to tell me, right? And being the doormat that I am, I wouldn't mind." Belle's voice was so lifeless. He couldn't imagine the hurt and betrayal she must be feeling.

"What are you talking about? Have you been sleep-walking again?" Laura was trying to play it off, but it seemed Belle had heard every word.

Belle was quiet almost too long. "At least you were right about one thing. I do make excuses for people, but I'm done making excuses for you."

"No, you're not. You are kind to a fault. All I have to do is cry awhile, beg forgiveness, and you'll forgive me. You always do." Laura was so calm it was eerie. Tristan wondered if she was a sociopath.

Belle shook her head. "No, Laura, I'm not. I don't hate you. I'm not angry, but we're done. I will not answer your calls. I will not come to your rescue. We are not friends. I don't care where you go or what you do, but you will be doing it without me. Consider this goodbye."

Laura's face fell, and she blinked like she was unable to process what was happening. "You're serious, aren't you?"

"Yeah. You should go." Belle looked at Tristan. "Do you mind if we talk a minute?"

He smiled. "No. Your room or mine?"

"I was thinking a lounge chair on the deck. Need to change?" She was talking to him like Laura wasn't even there.

"You're acting like this is over and I have no say in it," Laura said.

"Because it is, and you don't. Relationships are two-way streets. Unfortunately, yours always ran one way. To you. And I'm cutting you out of my life." Belle looked past her again and smiled at Tristan. "Fifteen minutes or are you moving slow?"

"Fifteen works." He winked and quickly went into his room, making sure to lock it behind him.

At least he got in his room without the crazy woman following him. He'd need to talk to his aunt about Laura too. He was pretty sure she was insane or something. Her behavior was beyond bizarre, and he had no idea what nutty thing she'd try. The one good thing about Belle seeing her true colors was that she wouldn't be barging in on them anymore.

If Belle hadn't panicked and called him her boyfriend when Paul and Laura showed up, who knows what would have happened. They may not have spent any time together, or not as much as they had. He wouldn't have gotten to know her. To see how beautiful her heart was, how strong she was, or any of the other wonderful things about her.

One day left at sea. One day left with her. He wasn't okay with that, but he knew they couldn't be together. She'd repeatedly said they could just be friends. They'd spend the day together, just the two of them, and he'd soak her up as much as he could until they docked in Miami.

LAURA'S JAW HUNG OPEN. Her eyes were glued to Belle, and it looked like she was shaking. It was an odd sight. "I can't believe you'd just cut me out."

"I can't believe you tried to seduce Tristan, used me, and expected me to be okay with it. I'm actually quite baffled at the moment. I'm wondering if you don't need therapy." Belle was done being a doormat where Laura was concerned. "What's especially crazy is the performance you gave during this cruise. Acting like you were sorry when you weren't sorry at all. More than likely, the only reason you kept pushing yourself on me was because I was with Tristan."

"I don't know what you're talking about."

Since her return from Felicia's office, her thoughts had been all over the place. Possibly having to pay the cruise line back, a deeper examination into her relationship with Laura, and realizing she was falling in love with Tristan. Not that she'd tell him that. He lived in Seattle, and she lived in Miami. It was a star-crossed thing, and those never ended well.

"Yeah, you do. You've played me since high school. I've spent this cruise going over our relationship. You were never my friend. Ever. I was your friend, and you abused me. I'm done." Belle squared her shoulders and held her head high. "Laura, I mean it this time. Don't come near me again. I'm done."

Laura actually looked shocked. "I've been staying with you since I broke it off with Paul. You can't just toss me out. I have nowhere to go."

"I suggest you go find Paul and work it out. Since he's the last man this carrot will be attracting." Belle turned and laid her hand on the door handle. "I really did love you; you know that. I don't know how long it'll take me to figure out what part of all of this hurts the most. I may never figure it out."

"Belle, come on. It's you. We're us. This is how we work. I do something or say something stupid, I ask for forgiveness, and we're friends again. That's how it's always worked." Laura tilted her head.

"No." She walked into her room, shut the door, and locked it. With a sigh, she slumped back on the door and slid down. Her heart felt like it had been cut in two, run down a cheese grater, and dropped into a bucket of alcohol. She didn't even know how to process what had happened.

When she'd walked to the door, it was because she heard Tristan in the hall. Finding Laura talking to him confused her. She'd left to get some ice, or that's what she'd told Belle. When she started telling Tristan all those things, a piece of her broke off and floated away.

Had other people used her like that? How did they do it and her not know it? Was she really that much of a doormat because she tried to put herself in other people's shoes? What was wrong with her? Tears pooled in her eyes. She'd been so stupid.

"Belle," Tristan called through the door. "The coast is clear." When she didn't answer, he called her name again.

She stood and opened the door. So what if he saw her crying? "Thanks."

He wiped her tears off with his thumb and tugged her to him. "I'm sorry. This cruise trip has been awful. I knew she was bad news from the beginning."

Awful? That was one way to look at it, but that's only if she looked at it like she'd lost her best friend all over again. Laura had never been her friend, but it did hurt. "I'd already come to the conclusion that once the cruise was over, our friendship was done. Honestly, deep down I knew it the moment she said you made a pass at her. Why didn't you say something?"

He pulled back and held her gaze. "I didn't want to come between your friendship, and I was afraid if I said anything, you'd push me away. Plus, I felt like that was a conclusion you needed to come to on your own."

"Good call. You ready to go?" He looked great in his dark-colored drawstring pajamas and white fitted shirt. He looked like a model. She pulled free and grabbed the blankets off her bed.

He paused a moment and rubbed the back of his neck. "Would you mind if I spread her ashes first? It's late, and I'm thinking there will be more privacy this way."

"I don't mind. I kinda figured that's what we were doing. Laura didn't need to know that, which is why I said find a lounge." She smiled.

"Thanks." He walked into his room, grabbed a small plain box and held it at his side. "I'm ready."

"Then let's go."

CHAPTER 18

"I don't know if I'm supposed to say something or what. I've never done this before." Tristan stood at the railing, looking out over the dark ocean water. They'd gone to the back section of the boat on the lowest deck and found it completely empty. He wasn't sure how he'd gotten so lucky, and he wasn't going to press his luck by asking.

Belle shrugged. "What do you *want* to do?"

"I don't know. I never thought about it. It was something she asked me to do; that's all." He looked down at the small box in his hand. Talk about perspective. It didn't matter who you were, how much money you had, or the power you yielded. When your life was over, you fit in a box. Ashes were ashes, and they were all gray.

Her small hand covered his as he held the box. "How about..." She took a deep breath. "My grandmother loved me and raised me when she didn't have to. I was little, angry, confused, and hurt because I'd lost my parents. She put up with me at my worst. And it's because of her I am who I am, because she loved me."

He wrapped his fingers around the top of the railing and gripped hard enough his knuckles turned white. "Yeah," he wanted to say, but the word was stuck in his throat.

Belle tiptoed, wiped his tears, and then put her arms around him. She said nothing else. All she did was hold him. What was strange was it was exactly what he needed. To stand on his grandmother's cruise ship at the railing, holding her ashes until he was ready to say goodbye one last time. How she knew that, how she knew him so well, was a mystery to him.

His grandmother would have been planning their wedding by now. She would have been taking him by the ear and telling him to do what it took to keep her. To tell her he'd fallen in love with her. He could almost hear her voice. *Nine days! Love doesn't have a date or time; it takes however long it takes. Nine hours, nine days, nine years...as long as when you do fall in love, you know they're the one.*

But life wasn't as simple or easy as his grandmother thought. There were too many variables. She didn't want a relationship, he didn't think she'd like his world, and they lived on opposite sides of the continent.

Tristan ran his fingers over the lid of the box. "I love you, Grandma." He pulled it open and watched his grandma's remains dance away on the air. Now he understood why she wanted it done on her cruise ship and at sea. One last time, she was full of life.

After, they found a lounger and cuddled under a blanket. He didn't realize how cold he was until then. Goosebumps covered him, and he shivered. "I know you have to be freezing too. You could have told me you were cold and then retreated under a blanket."

"No, I was where I was supposed to be. I'm fine. Cold, but fine."

She wasn't fine, but she sure was wonderful. "I know you aren't fine. I know finding out about Laura hurt. You may not believe me, but I understand more than you know how that feels."

"Strangely enough, I'm okay. I can't deny it: my heart did break when I heard the words come out of her mouth. I've been waiting for it to crater, but I think, down deep, I've known for a long time. I was just so hungry for friendship that I was willing to accept whatever scraps someone was willing to give me." She wiggled closer and tucked her hands under her chin. "I'm not willing to do that anymore. Not with her. Not with anyone. It's freeing, really, to know she isn't my responsibility anymore. I don't have to worry about whether she's happy, or whether I'm making her happy."

He curled his body around her as he tightened his hold on her. "You deserve better." Then he remembered what happened with his aunt after she left. Maybe hearing good news would help right about now. "By the way, you don't have to worry about paying the cruise line back. I gave my statement, and they're checking the video feed from that night in the elevator. I'm pretty sure Paul isn't going to like what they find."

Her lips parted, and she gasped. "I don't?" Her eyes watered as she smiled. "Oh, wow, thank you."

"He needed to get punched. I just wished it'd been me and not you. That way I would've had the satisfaction of decking him." It would have been satisfying—not smart, but definitely satisfying.

"It was actually therapeutic. Although, looking back, maybe I should have just keyed his Jag." She laughed. "I doubt he even felt it."

Tristan grunted. "Oh, he felt it. Maybe not a lot, but he got the point."

Belle turned quiet, and he wondered what she could be thinking. So much had happened in the short time they'd been on the cruise. The possibilities were endless.

"Would you tell me about your mom?" he asked.

Just when he thought she wasn't going to answer, she said, "She has Alzheimer's. It started in her early fifties. It started slow, so it was little things. By the time it was bad, it was really bad. It started with forgetting her keys, then it went to missing class times at the university, and then she got lost in the neighborhood we'd lived in since I was born. I knew something was wrong when I was nearly finished with my masters but she kept forgetting that I wasn't still in high school. That's when I finally convinced her to go to a doctor."

"I understand a little. My grandma didn't know me by the end. When did you decide she needed a nursing home?"

"Part of what got me while I was developing my campaign presentation was taking care of her. I had part-time care, and there was a twenty-minute gap from the time the nurse left until I got home from work." She paused and inhaled. "I was late getting home one evening, and I found her unconscious on the floor. She'd decided to clean our kitchen cabinets and fell off a chair. Or that's what I suspect. She was banged up and bruised, with a huge gash on her forehead. It was my fault because I'd cut corners."

"You were doing your best."

"It happened the night before I was supposed to do my presentation. So, yes, Paul was mostly to blame for my blowing it, but my personal life fell apart at the same time."

Tristan tipped her chin up with his finger. "You took care of her while going to college, didn't you?"

She nodded. "Part of the reason I graduated at twenty-six. I had to schedule my classes around her care. Then I got the job in Dallas, so we moved. Then I lost that job, which was awful, but coming to Miami six months ago was the best thing to happen. The nursing home here is the best in the city. I was lucky there was an opening."

"It sounds expensive."

"It is. I work two jobs to afford it, but it's worth it. Most of the time she doesn't remember me. Sometimes, she's violent. And that type of thing takes special people to work with them. Not everyone can be a nurse, and hers are the best." She held her bottom lip between her teeth. "You wouldn't want to...I mean...You know, never mind."

He chuckled. "You just had a conversation with me that I wasn't involved in. What are you trying to ask me?"

"You wouldn't want to go with me to see her, would you?" Her eyes darted to his and back down. "It's okay if you don't want to. I've put you on the spot. You know what; forget I asked."

Tristan tipped her chin up and covered her lips with his. He kissed her until she put her arm around his neck and buried her hands in his hair. He kissed her like his time was limited and he wanted to remember how she tasted. How she smelled. What it felt like to have her lips moving against his. He kissed her until she felt burned into his memory, and then he kissed her longer just to enjoy her.

When he came up for air, he nuzzled her neck with his nose and whispered, "I'd love to go with you."

Her breath was unsteady, and he could see the flush in her cheeks when he pulled back.

"Really?"

"Yeah." He wanted to meet the woman who had given the world Belle Evans. In his mind, she was owed a medal.

"Laura liked to act like she wanted to go with me, but she never did. Paul would look like he was going to throw up anytime I mentioned it. A nursing home can be depressing." She shrugged. "I can't not go see her. It doesn't matter if she remembers me, because I remember her and I just want one more day with her. Just one more day where she knows my name, that she's my mom. One more day to ask her advice on my career, my love life, or lack thereof. One more day. Just one more." The last three words were choked out. Tears streamed down her cheeks. She pressed her forehead to his chest and cried.

He held her until her soft cries stopped and she fell asleep. How long had she held that in? And then it hit him square in the chest. The people she loved didn't see her either. They saw what they wanted to see. Not the woman who was as strong as she was gentle.

They were so different, and yet, where it mattered, they were exactly the same. And he loved her but couldn't have her because she didn't want a relationship. And he wouldn't force himself on her. His chest tightened, and his heart felt like it was in a shirt press. He'd extended his time with her one extra day. Leaving was going to hurt him, and there was no way to prepare for it.

CHAPTER 19

Sunlight filtered through the small window in Belle's room as she stretched awake, and her hand bumped into something solid. She glanced over, and Tristan lay sound asleep on his stomach, arms hugging a pillow.

Their clothes were on, which was a good sign. That wasn't exactly something she would've wanted to be fuzzy on. She had to assume she'd fallen asleep and he'd brought her to her room. Only because he was Tristan, and that's what he'd do.

She gently caressed his cheek, and he inhaled, pressing his face into her hand. So this was what it would be like to wake up next to him. If she could remember falling asleep next to him, the dream would be complete.

He was everything she'd ever wanted, and she couldn't have him. He lived in Seattle. Besides, he'd been pretending to be her boyfriend. It didn't matter how real it all felt, it wasn't. Most of what they'd shared had been two people on a cruise, enjoying their time together. That was all.

What she did have was a full day at sea with him, and she would enjoy every second. Then she'd have him a little while on land when she went to see her mom. He would be the only person to ever visit with her.

Her family either lived too far away or they were estranged. Taking Tristan to see her mom would be like sharing a piece of herself. It made her pulse race. Maybe her mom would be having a good day. It had been months since she'd had a good day. She could hope Tristan would get a glimpse of the brilliant woman who'd raised her.

"Hi." His deep voice pulled her from her thoughts.

"Hey."

"What were you thinking about just then?" he asked as he pushed her hair back from her face.

Oh, he'd been watching her. Well, at least he hadn't caught her watching him, and she hadn't been drooling on him this time. That embarrassment would live with her for life. "I was thinking about my mom.

She doesn't have many good days anymore. The last time, it left me pretty torn."

"What happened?"

She smiled. "Oh, nothing. So, what's the plan today? It's the last day at sea. I'm thinking we—or you, Ashley, Maritsa, and Shawn—should play pool, and we could all hang out."

"I can be persuaded to do that, but only if you let me teach you to play. I bet with a little guidance, you won't be a deadly weapon." He smiled and tapped her on the nose.

She liked the idea of that. "Okay. We grab showers, get something to eat, and track them down."

"If they don't get to us first."

She chewed her bottom lip and smiled. "True." The temptation to kiss him had never been stronger. Morning had never been more welcomed. If she kissed him, she wouldn't want to stop, and that was a bad thing in a room where they wouldn't get interrupted.

Belle rolled off the bed and stood. "We're burning daylight."

Tristan stretched and sat up. "I hate to ask, but do you think Laura will try anything?"

Knowing Laura, she might as well flip a coin. "I don't know."

He stood and walked to her. "I haven't seen Paul since St. Thomas."

"Me either. Laura may have very well tried to make amends with him. She used me to find good men, or that's what she said. Joke was on her when I landed Paul." She laughed.

"I just want to make sure you're okay." He rubbed his hands up and down her arms.

She liked the comfort she felt when he was around. "I am."

"I'll see you in…"

This was the last day, and she wanted to look good. "How about thirty?"

"Thirty whole minutes?" he teased.

She rolled her eyes. "Twenty-five?"

"Deal." He kissed her forehead and strolled out of her room. The moment the door shut, she flopped on the bed like a kid with a crush. Only it wasn't a crush, she was head over heels in love with him.

For the first time since they'd received the diagnosis, she was angry with Alzheimer's for more than just taking her mom away. It was keeping her in Miami because her mom was in a good place. The disease was like wine on cotton, slowly spreading outward, staining everything it touched. It had broken her heart once, and it was coming back around to finish her off.

THE STEAMY WATER rolled over Tristan's shoulders and down his back, and he braced himself against the shower wall. His mind was a whirlwind of thought, and his emotions were all over the place.

He'd woken up to Belle lying next to him. After she'd fallen asleep, he'd brought her to her room and put her to bed. When he went to leave, she'd asked him to stay, and saying no wasn't a strength he had. Not when it came to her.

She'd been so lost in thought, he'd had the opportunity to lie next to her and stare. He was glad she didn't realize it and determine he was a creep or weirdo. He liked being near her, and he knew their time together was coming to a close.

Her suggestion that they spend time with Shawn, Maritsa, and Ashley caught him off guard. He'd hoped they'd spend it alone together, but teaching her to play pool would be fun. It almost felt like a public service after the way she'd played.

Hot water was supposed to be good at helping stress and tension, but it hadn't helped him at all. No matter how long he stood there, thoughts about Belle were going to keep him wound tight.

He turned the water off and threw a towel around

his waist. A light tapping came from the door, and he wondered who it could be. He strode to the door and opened it.

Belle's eyes went wide, and she spun around. "Uh, I, um, um…I thought you'd be ready. I'm sorry."

"You said twenty-five minutes." She was too cute. Her cheeks had gone from creamy-white to apple-red in seconds.

"I changed my mind."

"All right, give me five or less." He shut the door and quickly dressed. When he stepped out, she still had her back to the door. "I'm dressed. You can turn around now."

She glanced over her shoulder at him. The color in her cheeks had lessened, but it wasn't gone. "Really. Answering the door in a towel?"

He hadn't even thought about it. "I was covered."

"Not enough," she murmured. Her cheeks lit up again.

It was fun making her blush. "You're cute when you blush."

"That wasn't nice. Not bad either, but not nice at all." She slapped a hand over her mouth and turned away.

Tristan tried not to laugh but couldn't hold it in.

She whirled around and smacked him in the gut. "That's not nice either."

"I'm sorry."

Then her entire demeanor changed. She lifted on her tiptoes and brushed her lips along his jaw. Her fingers walked up his chest and threaded through his hair. In an instant, nothing was funny. His pulse had gone from a normal to full throttle in the span of a heartbeat.

She skimmed her lips across his cheek and stopped just as she reached his lips, where she hovered so close it was torture. "Not so funny when it's happening to you, huh?"

Message received. He swallowed hard and tugged her to him. "You do not play fair."

"Hey, you answered the door in a towel. I wasn't expecting that."

"You...you..." What could he say? She made him want to forget why they couldn't be together, to whisk her away, and forget the world existed.

She tilted her head. "I what?"

No, he couldn't say that. "Nothing. I'm hungry. Are you ready to go?"

Belle placed the palm of her hand against his chest and kissed him. "I'm ready now."

CHAPTER 20

"Oh, guys, this was so fun. I'm sad it's over. Whatever those marketing guys want, I'll give it to them. I had the best time ever," Maritsa said and kissed Shawn.

Belle was trying to listen, but Tristan was curled around her as she hunched over the pool table, showing her how to hold a pool cue and shoot the ball without killing anyone.

His lips were against her ear, driving her nuts. "Okay, you don't want to hit it hard. You want to tap it." He kept his hands over hers as she hit the cue ball. It rolled forward, and the rest of the pool balls split apart. If her hand hurt, she wasn't aware of it.

The group cheered, and elation zipped through her. "I did it. Well, you did it. I was just kinda there."

"No, I only gave a little support. It was all you." He hugged her from behind, and she reveled in it.

Tristan was a wall of warmth, security, and comfort. It was going to be hard going back to being alone. It would be her in her little rundown trailer in a mobile home park, working two jobs and paying the nursing home almost every dime she made.

Staying ahead meant she didn't have to worry when there wasn't enough work at the diner, or when there were unpaid days off at the office. There was a cushion, and it gave her peace of mind.

"It's your turn again," Tristan said.

She lifted her head and smiled. "Okay. I'm a little nervous. I don't want to hurt anyone."

Everyone took a step back and laughed.

"Very funny. All of you. You're just hilarious." She rolled her eyes and leaned over the pool table. *Just tap it*. Her hands shook as she drew the stick back and thrust it forward. A full-on cheer erupted from the group when the ball stayed on the table. She didn't sink any, but for her, it was a little victory all the same. "Yes!" She twisted around and pumped her fist in the air.

"That was awesome," Maritsa said. "He's a good teacher."

What she wanted to say was, "No, he's just good.

All the way down. He is decent, sweet, and kind. Everything a good man should be." Instead, she nodded her head and smiled at him. "Yeah, he is."

He winked at her and shot her a half-smile. "I knew you could do it."

"You're the only one." She giggled.

Tristan put his arm around her waist and kissed the top of her head. "I doubt it."

Why did the cruise have to end? Or why couldn't it have been eighteen days? No, that would have been worse. How much more broken-hearted would she be if she had nine more days of him and then had to let him go?

"Okay, let's finish this game now that we know we're safe," Maritsa teased.

Belle narrowed her eyes. "You're on."

They played several more games, and for the first time in a long while, she felt like she was in the company of people who could be lifetime friends. Being on this cruise hadn't been the best ever, only because of everything that happened. It had taught her a lot though. It had given her memories she'd hold on to forever. One of them being Tristan.

He was worth all the Pauls and Lauras in the world. She would cherish the time she had with him, and now she had proof that there were good guys out there. Ones that were loyal and didn't cheat. Tristan was worth more to her than the entire trip.

AFTER PLAYING pool most of the afternoon, Tristan was able to steal Belle away from the group. He enjoyed playing and hanging out, but he wanted time alone with her. In twenty-four hours, actually less, he'd be heading back to Seattle. He didn't want to share what little time left he had with her.

"You know, for cruise food, this was pretty good. I haven't had anything I didn't like," Belle said. "I wonder what kind of questions they'll ask us before we leave."

He'd ordered room service, and they were having dinner in his room. That was one way to make sure he didn't have to deal with interruptions. "No clue, but I'll be able to honestly say, 'This was the best cruise I've ever been on.'"

"I could have done without Paul, finding out my best friend was never my best friend, and getting sick. Otherwise, it was fantastic," she said and finished her strawberry shortcake. "*That* was awesome. I almost want to lick the plate."

"You did kind of devour it."

Her eyes widened. "Oh, I was supposed to share it." She covered her face with her hands. "I'm so sorry."

"If I wanted any, I would have intervened," he said through a laugh.

She peeked between her fingers. The pink on her cheeks was showing through as well. "I'm so embarrassed."

"Don't be." She was too cute.

She dropped her hands to her lap. "Want to take a walk? It's our last night on board, and I think I'm going to miss the ocean air."

"Find a lounge and watch the stars in our finest pajamas?"

Her hair bounced around her shoulders as she nodded. "I'll get the blankets and get dressed."

What adorable set of pajamas was she going to wear tonight? "Okay. You can't need more than ten minutes."

She shook her head. "Nope."

Belle left, and he switched clothes. He'd never changed so fast. Or he thought so. She was waiting for him when he came out of his room. This time she was wearing light-green bottoms with tacos on them and a top that read, "There's no wrong time for a taco."

A laugh popped out before he could stop it.

She narrowed her eyes, but her lips curved into a smile. "Are you laughing at my pajamas?"

There was no way to lie. "Yes. They're cute."

"They're old but comfortable."

"Mine are too." That was kind of true. He wasn't sure when he got them, or if he'd ever worn them before.

Her eyebrows shot up. "Those are old? They look brand new. You must really take care of your clothes. I wish I could do that. Maybe my stuff wouldn't look so faded."

She looked good in everything, faded or not. "You look great. And these I found buried in a drawer. There is a possibility I've never worn them before because I forgot about them."

"I did that with a shirt once, but by the time I found it, it was too small. I tried it on and almost got stuck in it. It wasn't that tight going on, but coming off, it was a straightjacket."

He tried picturing it but failed. "It couldn't have been that bad."

"Oh, no, it was. I almost used scissors until I managed to get one arm out. I put that thing in the donation bin faster than I could blink." Belle nodded to the elevator as it opened. "I think it's calling to us."

They hurried down the hall, onto the elevator, and

out to the deck. It wasn't as empty as the night before, but it was empty enough that they found a lounge away from everyone else.

It wasn't as cold as the previous night, but that didn't keep them from bundling up and cuddling under the blanket.

"This, I could do all the time. Sit out under the stars on the ocean with..." Belle stopped. "A good friend."

"Just a good friend?" He shouldn't be pushing it, but the question just popped out.

Belle spread her hand on his chest and looked up at him. "I think that's probably the best place to leave it."

"What if we didn't have to?"

Sadness flashed in her eyes. "You live in Seattle. I live here. My mom is in a good place, and moving her again would be bad. Plus, we've known each other nine days. Good friends, that's better than where we started. And if we leave it there, then nothing can go wrong."

He knew he was pushing it, but he couldn't stop himself. "But what if—"

She touched her fingers to his lips. "'What if' leads to confusion and hurt. Let's enjoy the last night and just be in the here and now."

Maybe she didn't feel about him the way he felt

about her. That was a possibility. That's not the feeling he got from her, but she was sweet. And she had been upfront about not wanting to be in a relationship. Just because they kissed and he felt a connection didn't mean she felt the same.

Here and now. That's what she wanted, and that's what he'd give her. He needed to listen to what she was saying without words. "Okay. No more questions."

Her fingers were replaced with her lips and feathery kisses. He kissed her back with the same gentleness until he couldn't take it, deepening the kiss and tightening his hold on her. He would never love anyone as much as he loved her. He kissed her, hoping she was listening to what he wasn't saying with words, and he hoped she understood what each kiss meant.

CHAPTER 21

It was time to pack up and disembark before Belle was ready. It was her birthday, but she sure didn't feel thirty. Spending the previous night with Tristan on the deck was like getting a birthday cake with a million candles, and the morning felt like she was blowing them out. Why did it have to end?

Why did he have to ask those questions last night? It only made her wish things could be different. People couldn't live across the country from one another and have a relationship, especially when one of those people had two jobs and spare moments were spent visiting their mom.

Still, she couldn't shake the questions. What if they could be together? What if they could make it work?

What if he could move to Miami? Or if she could move to Seattle? Would it work if they continued to see each other?

She sure did love him. There was no doubt about that. If she asked, would he move? What if she asked and he said no? What if she asked and he said yes? Would she be able to make him happy? She lived in a run-down trailer in a dump of a trailer park. She worked all the time. It wouldn't be fair to ask him to move for her if she was never going to be around. She wouldn't be able to give him what he needed.

There were no second chances in life. What if he was her chance to be with someone she loved? Did he love her though? He sure kissed her like he did, or at least like it was a possibility.

She smacked her forehead with her hand and shook her head. It was stupid to think all this stuff. Pushing all the nagging questions out of her mind, she finished packing and met Tristan, along with the other winners, in the large dining hall.

"Good morning." Tristan tugged her close and kissed her.

Oh, why did he have to smell so good and look so good? Dark dress slacks, a light-blue dress shirt, and a smile that could light up Chicago. If she had a kryptonite, it was him and his gorgeous smiles. "Hey."

"You look beautiful this morning."

In faded jeans and an even more faded shirt? Right. He was definitely being nice today. "Yeah, right. I saved the worst outfit for last."

He kissed her cheek again. "Your outfits have nothing to do with your beauty."

Cripes. Her heart was already pounding, and his sweet nothings were only making it pound harder. "Head. Bands."

Tristan threw his head back and laughed. "I said I'd take care of that."

"Hey, guys," Ashley said as she walked up with Maritsa and Shawn. "We're going to have brunch after we dock. Kind of like a farewell thing. Would you be interested?"

"Um…" Belle didn't mind as long as it was cheap.

"That sounds great. My treat though," Tristan said. "It's Belle's birthday."

"Really?" Ashley asked. "Then it's a definite. We'll all chip in."

Belle was thrilled he remembered her birthday, but pointed nails slowly raked down a chalkboard. She felt the color drain from her face. No, he couldn't pay. Not for her. She didn't want her last day with him to be ruined, and the memory of their day in San Juan was playing in full color. "That's okay. I'll pay for myself."

"It's fine." He looked at her like he was reading her mind. "I willingly offered to pick up the tab for the whole group."

He bent down and whispered, "Belle, it's okay. I promised you I wouldn't do that again, and I meant it."

"But you don't remember how you were looking at me," she whispered back.

He leaned back and held her gaze. "Yes, I do, and it will never happen again."

"Nah, if it's her birthday, we'll go to my restaurant. My Yaya has the best food and desserts." Maritsa grinned. "It'll be my treat."

She'd told them about her family's Cuban infused restaurant, and from the sound of it, it was something Belle wanted to try. She relaxed. It was okay if it was Maritsa's treat. "Okay."

Tristan looked hurt. "Sure."

It broke her heart. She hated seeing him sad. Taking his hand, she whispered, "You're right. You did say it would never happen again. I'm sorry I hurt you."

He held her gaze and smiled. "It's okay."

Maritsa lifted on her toes and craned her neck. "Oh, looks like we're on."

The final meeting was more like an opinion panel than an interview. The winners, along with a few of the paying passengers, were seated, and they would raise their hand or offer a comment here and there. It took about an hour, and then half of them were released. The other half would stay for promotional photos.

They didn't pick Belle to stay, and she was sure it had something to do with her outfit. She wasn't exactly the clientele they were hoping to reach: broke and never coming back. They did pick Tristan, Ashley, Maritsa, and Shawn, which left her with some time to kill.

She pulled her luggage behind her as she walked down the ramp to the pier. Once they were all finished, she'd be meeting them so they could follow each other to the restaurant.

Belle stopped midway as Laura came into view. After not seeing her the day before, she was hoping she wouldn't ever see her again. She closed her eyes and took a deep breath.

Since there was no point in delaying it and she really didn't want an audience, she walked the rest of the way down the ramp and stopped in front of Laura.

"Belle, can we talk?" Laura asked.

"There's nothing to talk about." Whatever friendship she had with her was over. There was no ground to build on. Laura had used a nuclear weapon and destroyed it.

Laura tucked a piece of hair behind her ear. "Please, can you just give me five minutes?"

What could Laura say in five minutes that would change her mind? Nothing.

Laura looked down. "Please."

"Okay. You've got five minutes and not a second more."

They were a few feet from the ramp, away from anyone who could overhear. "Okay, talk," Belle said and looked at her watch. She was giving her exactly five minutes.

"Were you serious the other night? About us not being friends anymore?" Laura asked.

Okay, she was seriously bonkers. How had Belle never seen that before? Because she made excuses for her. "Yeah, I was serious, Laura. Is that all?"

Laura leveled her eyes at her. The previous demure looks she had given Belle were gone, and now she was looking at her like she could claw her eyes out. "You really think billionaire Tristan Stone wants you? Because that's who's been your pretend boyfriend during this cruise. That's who you've been spending your time with. That's who's been kissing you. He may have thought that facial hair could fool most people, but it didn't fool me."

Belle was shocked he was a billionaire, but she

didn't care about any of that. He was good and kind. She loved him. "His name is Tristan Davis," she said.

"His *name* is Tristan Stone. Not only does he run a Fortune 500 company, he inherited this cruise company from his grandmother. I bet the only reason he was here was to check out how things were going, what needed to be improved. Only to find the most gullible woman on board and make her think he could actually fall in love with her. And it would have to be little ole you!" She crossed her arms over her chest and sneered.

Of course, Laura would retaliate. It was her style. Why did she agree to talk to her? "Your five minutes are up." Belle turned to leave. Tristan wasn't like that, and Belle knew it. Laura was just spewing venom because she was vindictive.

Laura's lips curled into a snarl. "Think about what I said, Belle. Think about his world. Fancy clothes, dinners, exotic places…Wealth you couldn't begin to imagine. Do you really think you belong in his world? The girl who lives in a shack while working two jobs, taking care of her mindless mother?"

The last few words left her heart in shards. Her composure wavered a second. She didn't know how Laura knew where she lived, but she didn't care at this point. "Yeah, but at least I won't be taking care of you, and that's worth something." Belle turned, and the group was staring in her direction.

"Yeah, and you won't be taking care of him either, because you aren't good enough. He knows it, and you know it." Laura smacked into her shoulder as she walked around her and left.

She'd never seen Tristan Stone. She didn't follow celebrity gossip or read society news. So he was Tristan Stone, and she knew it was true. Laura wouldn't lie about that. Belle wondered why he hadn't felt he could tell her himself. She understood trying to blend in, but she hoped he would've felt comfortable enough to tell her by now. What reason did he have not to tell her? Did he not trust her?

The new revelation definitely squashed the what if's she'd asked herself earlier. Not that she thought he was that shallow or that she believed what Laura said. She would be good to him; she would just never fit in his world. He needed tall, well-dressed women who knew how to throw dinner parties and loved caviar. Just thinking about all the people who would expect things from her was overwhelming.

The cruise was over, and real life had already struck. Her glass slipper was two sizes too small, and her pumpkin was rotting. Belle steeled herself and pasted on a smile as she met the group.

Tristan's lips were pursed. "Are you okay?"

Maritsa hugged her. "Girl, you are as pale as white bread."

"What did she say to you?" asked Shawn.

"Nothing of importance, just mean-spirited things." The last thing she wanted was sympathy or anyone feeling sorry for her, especially Tristan.

Tristan put his arms around her and leaned down to whisper, "What did she say?"

Nothing she wanted to tell Tristan Stone, the billionaire. "Things I'd rather not repeat," she whispered back. It wasn't that he was a billionaire. It was that Laura was right about one thing. His world was so far from hers that it would never work.

CHAPTER 22

*B*elle was glad she was driving something decent. Her seven-year-old Ford pickup was a little dented here and there from the move, but that was just the hazards of driving. It wasn't falling apart, nor did it have mismatched paint and rust.

"I have to admit, I didn't expect you to be driving a truck." He chuckled. "It's nice too."

"I used it to move here. I had a newer car, but it wouldn't have held what I needed. So I traded it in. This is the product of job number three. After I got it paid off, I quit." She glanced at him as she drove.

"Three jobs?" His jaw dropped. "Wow. How did you manage three jobs?"

She shrugged. "You do what you have to do."

Silence filled the single cab truck long enough to make her squirm.

Tristan twisted in the seat. "Are you sure you're okay?"

She nodded. "Yeah, I'm fine." Nothing about who he was had changed except his name. Why did Laura have to do that? What had Belle done to her that was so awful that she needed to tell her who he was? She may have found out eventually, but it would have been after he left, hopefully.

He reached across the seat and took her hand. "Belle, it feels like something has changed, but it hasn't. Nothing has changed."

She pulled the pickup into a spot at the restaurant and looked at him. "No, it hasn't." They still couldn't be together, especially now that she knew who he was. He couldn't leave Seattle. He was running a company. People with jobs depended on him. People like her.

"Okay."

They got out of the car and met up with Ashley, Maritsa, and Shawn at the door of Maritsa's restaurant.

Maritsa held Shawn's hand as she smiled. "My Yaya isn't here today, but the food will still be great."

Tristan looked over his shoulder. "The place is packed."

Maritsa lifted an eyebrow. "Of course it is. This is the best food in Miami. Come on. We do family style here. I've got a table ready. Order whatever you want. Don't be shy. And I'll know, so don't make me order for you."

Man, she had attitude and then some. Belle really liked her. She wished Laura hadn't been so intrusive so they could've spent more time together.

Tristan placed his hand on the small of Belle's back, and it felt as natural as breathing. They walked through the restaurant and sat at a large round table.

"Holy smokes, it smells good," Ashley said. "I think I want one of everything."

Maritsa giggled. "How you think I got my big butt?"

Shawn whispered something in her ear, and she kissed him like no one was watching.

Tristan leaned over and put his lips to Belle's ear. "I don't know what he said, but whatever it was, it was the right thing to say."

Belle chuckled. "Yeah, no kidding."

After they'd checked out the menu and asked Maritsa some questions, they all ordered. Once the waiter was gone, their conversation started back up.

"Where do you guys work?" asked Tristan.

Ashley rolled her eyes. "I work downtown for a

lawyer's office. I'm working to get my Paralegal Associate's Degree."

"I work here," Maritsa said. "On Fridays there's live music. We're doing well and getting recognition. My Yaya knows how to cook, so I knew it'd be huge."

Shawn smiled wide. "I'm a professional surfer. I haven't hit it big yet, but I'm supposed to sign a deal with a major company this week. I can't say who because it's going to be a huge announcement."

Tristan's eyes went wide, and his mouth dropped open. "I knew I recognized you. You were at the Triple Crown in Oahu. That wave was insane, and you just owned it."

"Yeah, that was me."

Belle hadn't seen him so animated. Apparently, Tristan's love of surfing hadn't lessened as much as he thought. "I didn't know you still followed surfing."

"Oh, well, not like religiously or anything, but I enjoy going when I'm able. If you ladies get the chance, you really should watch this guy sometime. He's incredible." Tristan looked at Shawn. "I'm surprised it took this long for a company to sign you."

Maritsa smiled and snuggled closer to Shawn. "That's my man."

"Thanks." Shawn's face was red, and he looked both embarrassed and thrilled.

"How about you, Belle? Where you do you work?" Ashley asked.

Did she tell them about both jobs or just the one that wasn't absolutely horrible? "I work in a CPA office as an administrative assistant."

"That's not too bad," Shawn said. "I did that before my surfing career took off. My dad's a CPA, so I had an in. But it was still okay work."

Belle nodded. "No, it's not bad." It was also not what she loved, but it paid the bills...almost.

Their waiter returned with their orders and checked their drinks. "If you need anything else, just let me know." The man smiled and walked off.

For the next few hours, the group ate and chatted. Maritsa insisted they agree to get together to eat or hang out from time to time. Belle found herself wanting that. Not having Laura around was giving her a new way to see things. These people were genuinely interested in things she said. They didn't talk over her or see through her. They didn't try to hog the attention or make snide comments. The people sitting around her were people she could call friends. It made her feel good.

When it came time for dessert, every possible thing on the menu was delivered, and the entire restaurant sang happy birthday to her. She'd never been more embarrassed or happy. Real friends. That's what real friendship felt like.

When they were full and talked out, they said their goodbyes. They'd exchanged numbers, and Tristan even gave Belle his. She'd delete it when he left. If she could muster the courage.

TRISTAN LOOKED out the window of Belle's pickup. They'd left Maritsa's restaurant and traveled to the opposite side of Miami. It stung that she hadn't been willing to let him buy her a birthday meal. That day in San Juan had hit her harder than he thought. Was there a way to repair the mistrust? "Belle, I need to ask you something, and I need you to be honest."

"Okay."

"Are you ever going to forgive me for what I did in San Juan?"

She sighed. "I have forgiven you. It's just that you talk about people using you. I don't want to ever be lumped in with them."

He didn't think that at all. She'd been so completely opposite that there was no way he could ever think of her like that. "I don't think of you like that. I offered to buy because I wanted to, not because I felt obligated or anything."

"I know, but I can pay my own way." She gave him a side glance. "Your offer was sweet and generous. It was nice of you."

"But you won't let me do anything nice for you." Truth be told, she'd hurt his feelings by wanting to pay for herself.

She stopped at a traffic light and turned to him. "But you have. You showed me what it's like to be treated well. You pretended to be dating me just so I didn't look pathetic to an ex. You didn't hit on Laura. You bought me this beautiful ring and a massage. I got to spend time with you. Just you being you was nice."

"But paying for the food was being me too."

The light turned green, and she drove on. "I'm so sorry I hurt your feelings. It was not my intent. I guess I was just scared that you'd walk away again, and I've only got a few hours left with you."

"I guess we both have fears we need to get over." Tristan paused, and before he could finish, her phone rang.

She grabbed it and put it to her ear. "Hello?...Oh, yeah, I'm so sorry...I'll bring it when I come." She ended the call and set the phone down. "I need to run by my house and grab something for the nursing home. They want me to fill out this thing for financial assistance. I've told them she won't qualify, but they are insistent."

"Why doesn't she qualify?"

"I didn't realize what was going on with her until things were bad. All of her retirement was gone, and I don't know where it went. She'd hidden the foreclosure notices from me." She stopped at another traffic light and looked at him. "She's not old enough for government assistance. I've told them all that. I guess they just needed it filled out to check it off their list."

"I'm sorry."

"Don't be. It's life." She paused. "I'm going to need you to do me a favor, okay?"

A favor? "Okay." He braced himself. Whatever it was, he would trust that she cared about him.

She took a left when a green arrow flashed and glanced at him. "When I tell you, I need you to close your eyes and keep them closed until I tell you to open them again, okay?"

The weirdest favor he'd ever been asked, by far. "Why?"

"Because I don't want you to see where I live. I don't want anyone's pity or anything. Things are the way they are, and that's all there is to it." She slowed the truck down. "Now, close your eyes."

Tristan looked around. The paved street had run out, and they were on a dirt road. It was overgrown with vegetation, and it'd rained recently.

"Please."

Where on earth was she taking him, and why were banjos playing in his head? "Okay," he said and closed his eyes.

They drove a few more minutes, and she parked. "I'm leaving the truck on because I won't be gone long. Keep. Your. Eyes. Closed." She kissed his cheek, and he heard the door open and shut.

He counted to twenty and peeked. "Oh..." How could she live there? The paint on the little blue trailer was peeling, several of the windows were boarded up, and it looked like it'd been put together with duct tape. He clamped his eyes shut as the trailer door opened, but the place was just as vivid.

She lived in that? He loved her. How was he going to let her continue living in that shack? He didn't feel sorry for her; he felt an overwhelming need to take care of her. Not because she needed it, but because he loved her and wanted to. How could he get her out of that place without her fighting him tooth and nail? If he said anything, she'd know he'd opened his eyes.

The door opened and shut again. "You peeked, didn't you?"

"What? No."

"Tristan Davis. I can see it on your face." He could feel her staring at him.

He shook his head. "I was just thinking about things. That's all."

"I know you aren't telling the truth. Don't think I don't know. I know it's bad, but it's what I can afford. And no, you can't help me. I've got it." She took his face in her hands. "I'm fine. I have a good life. I have a roof over my head, food in my cupboards, and my mom is in a nursing home where I don't have to worry."

Tristan slowly opened his eyes. "I'm sorry I peeked. I couldn't help it."

"It's not as bad as it looks. My neighbors are just poor, not evil. They're hard-working, kind, and they look out for me. Don't worry, okay?" She kissed him and then buckled her seatbelt. "You ready to meet my mom?"

"Absolutely." That was all he could say. He didn't have words for the other things he was feeling, and even if he did, he wasn't sure he could express them. For now, he'd push away the image of that hole she called a home and concentrate on the present and the time he had left.

CHAPTER 23

Gloria Jenkins gathered Belle into a hug, squeezed, and released her. "Oh, it is good to see you. How was your cruise?" Then she looked at Tristan. "Honey, was he a parting gift?"

His cheeks turned red, and Belle pointed a finger at him. "See, not nice." She giggled. "This is my friend Tristan. I met him on the cruise."

Her eyebrows hitched up. "Oh."

"It's not like that." Belle needed the topic to change. "How is she?"

The woman's lips curved down, and the happy expression turned somber. "She has her moments of clarity, but it's not getting any better. I don't know if she'll recognize you today."

"That's okay. As long as I get to see her, I'm good."

That wasn't true, but there was no point in breaking down in front of Tristan. She'd roped him into being her pretend boyfriend, he'd dealt with Paul and Laura, she'd drooled on him, cried on him, and now she had him at a nursing home.

What in the world was she thinking, inviting him here? She turned to him. "You know, you really don't have to come. It's depressing, and I shouldn't have asked."

He tangled his fingers in hers. "Let's go."

"I'll see you on the way out," Gloria said.

They walked together down the hall, took a right, and stopped six doors down. "I've never done this before."

"It's fine. I want to meet her."

She looked at the floor. "I just don't know what to expect."

He tipped her chin up. "Let's go see your mom."

Oh, why did she have to meet him? Why did he have to be so wonderful?

She turned the knob, and they stepped inside. "Mama? It's me, Belle."

The hospital bed was angled up, and the TV was on. "Who?" Her mom turned her head and squinted. She was wearing an outfit she'd worn when she was a professor: a dark-blue blazer, a light-blue blouse, and a pencil skirt that matched the blazer. Her hair was combed straight and parted on the side. It had gotten longer and now sat on her shoulders.

"It's Belle. You remember? I'm your daughter."

Her mom looked Tristan up and down. "And who's that? Is he my son?"

"No, Mama. He's my friend." Belle approached the bed with Tristan following her. "This is Tristan Davis. I went on a cruise and met him. He's nice."

"Nice? That's good." Her mom flipped the channel a few times.

"Tristan, this is Donna Evans. She was the Dean of Physics. She's brilliant."

Her mom eyed her. "You stop bragging, young lady. It's a sign of weakness to brag. Our strength comes from people seeing who we are, not in us telling them."

"Yes, Momma." Belle hung her head. No matter how old she got, it was never fun getting chastised by her mom.

"How are you feeling?" Tristan asked.

Her mom leaned back and looked at him. "I'm fine. How are you feeling?"

"I'm feeling pretty good. It's nice to meet you."

Her mom stuck her hand out and shook his hand. "It's nice to meet you too."

"Have you had a good day?" he asked.

"Well, I won Jeopardy, so yeah." Her mom smiled.

Tristan laughed. "I've never seen it."

"Never seen it? You look smart; you should watch it. Smart people watch Jeopardy." Her mom was laying on the charm. Belle was glad she was having a good moment.

"I'll have to remember that."

Her mom squinted her eyes again and looked at Belle. "You're Belle."

"Yes, Momma." Oh no, the moment was ending. She just needed a little more time.

"My daughter."

"Yes, Momma."

Her momma's lips curled, and she lunged for Belle. Tristan grabbed her around her waist and moved her out of reach. If he hadn't, her mom would've had her by the hair. The last time was bad enough.

She threw the remote and nearly hit Tristan. "I don't know you. Get out. GET OUT! I don't know you!" Her mom began screaming, and Belle darted out of the room.

Gloria was already running toward the room. "She did this earlier. We'll get her calmed down if you want to try again."

"She's done that before?" Tristan asked.

"Behavioral changes. She can be violent at times. It's not her fault. It's the disease. It's slowly eating her mind. One day, she won't know who I am and she'll never remember me again. That's why I visit. Because I know that day is coming, and I don't want to miss the times she remembers me."

He touched her cheek. "I can't imagine how hard it is for you. She is brilliant though. You could see it in her eyes."

The words struck her hard. He'd seen it, and she knew he wouldn't lie to her. Someone had seen her mom for who she was and not what the disease was doing to her. "Thank you for that."

"It's the truth."

The visit was over, and so was her time with him. She needed to get him to the airport before she wanted to keep him forever. Well, she already wanted to do that. What she didn't need was jail time because she used handcuffs. "I guess we should go."

"My flight doesn't leave until after dinner. Would you have dinner with me? I owe you a birthday dinner." He grinned.

Belle shook her head. "I don't know."

"You mean you'd dump me at the airport and make me sit there by myself? All alone? For hours?" He was working the puppy dog eyes.

She couldn't stop the smile from spreading on her lips. "That's not nice."

"Please."

Oh geez, he was killing her. What could she wear? How would she change? She couldn't take him back home.

"How about somewhere sit down but not super fancy?" he asked.

It was like he was reading her mind. He was taking away all her reasons to say no. "Okay. There's a steak place about four miles from here. Peanuts on the floor, the best bread I've ever eaten, and the steaks are fantastic. It's not too expensive either. Well, for steaks at least."

He smiled like he'd won the lottery. Or won it a few times. Did billionaires play the lottery? "Okay, let's go."

Ugh. He was so happy and kissable. He had to stop being so dang kissable. It was a good thing they were in public. Belle had no choice but to keep her wits and her lips to herself.

She took a last look inside her mom's room, and Gloria shook her head. Her visit with her mom was officially over. She wished it could have lasted longer, but that's how the visits were nowadays. Short, and most of the time she'd turn violent at the end.

"Is she okay?" he asked.

"She's okay. Our visit is just over." She let the door close and smiled as she looked at him.

He touched her arm. "I'm sorry."

"Me too." She needed to go before she started crying. That's what happened most of the time: her driving home, crawling into bed, and crying herself to sleep. A deep breath, a ten count, and she could keep it together a while longer. "If you're ready, I am too."

"Okay, lead the way." He smiled.

THE VISIT with Belle's mom was shorter than he could have predicted. Her mom was talking, and everything seemed fine. Then he saw the twitch in her arm, and he knew something had changed. The way her mother's face twisted would stick with him for a long time. It had to hurt her, visiting someone she loved who was so unpredictable.

Belle sat across from him, pushing her food around on her plate. The restaurant was just as she described: crushed peanuts underfoot, warm chewy bread, and seasoned steaks that hit the spot.

"Penny for your thoughts?" he asked.

She smiled as she lifted her head. "Nah, I don't have change."

"Funny. What were you thinking about?"

Her face was a mask, and he had no idea what was about to come out of her mouth. "Nothing, really. Tell me about where you live. You saw mine."

How did he tell her without giving away who he was? Why was he still holding on to it so tightly anyway? Because he liked being just Tristan. It was the first time he'd felt like a regular guy in a long time. "I live in a condo." He left the penthouse part off.

"Oh, well, I bet that's nice. Not sure about the HOA fees, but you don't have to cut your grass or deal with maintenance. Do you like your neighbors?" She set her fork down and stared at him.

"They're okay. They keep to themselves." Because he didn't have any. His condo took up the entire top floor.

She nodded. "That's good. Mine do too, for the most part. Mr. Richards is kind of a nosy guy. There are both advantages and disadvantages to that. My place is being watched, and my place is being watched. I have no doubt he'll be asking about the guy in my truck tomorrow."

"I can see that having positives and negatives," he said and sat back. "Will you tell me what Laura said?

Something's been different ever since you spoke to her."

Belle cast her gaze down to the table and chewed her bottom lip. He could see the debate raging on her face. "She said I wasn't good enough for you. That I would never be good enough for you."

It was a good thing he hadn't found that out when Laura was around. "You know that's not true."

"I do, but there's some truth to it. I work two jobs, and I visit my mom every spare second I have. It wouldn't be fair to be in a relationship with someone and have no time for them. You're kind and sweet. You should have someone who has the ability to spend time with you." She smiled, but it was thin and tight.

He narrowed his eyes. "That's not all she said, is it?"

"The other things she said were stupid and aren't worth repeating."

Tristan knew that wasn't all. If he were a betting man, he'd bet she knew who he was and she wasn't going to admit it. He wondered why. Most women would have jumped at the opportunity to divulge that they knew. Why not her? "Are you sure that's all?"

"I'm sure." She held his gaze and didn't blink an eye. "Do you have any family on your father's side, aside from your grandmother?"

Man, she was good at turning it back on him. "I

have an aunt, my dad's sister. We're pretty close. Not as close as me and my grandma, but not far."

"Do you have a big family on your mom's side?"

"Mid-size. We'd fit in a large SUV." He chuckled. "I have several cousins, mostly women, or they are now. How about you? You've never mentioned your dad. Where is he?"

Her cheeks turned red. "That's a bit of a weird story."

"This I have to hear." What kind of story could turn her that red?

She sighed and leaned forward on the table. "My mom didn't want to get married, but she wanted a child. So, she looked through a profile catalog and chose him."

"Oh." He thought about it a second. Then it dawned on him what she was saying. "Ohhh...she...oh."

"She liked his intelligence, his looks, and his winning personality." She grinned wide, showing her teeth.

He didn't want to laugh, but there was no containing it. "I'm so sorry. It's not funny. I swear it's not."

Belle shrugged. "It's okay. I've had worse reactions. Believe me."

"I would have never guessed that at all." Of all the things he'd imagined, that wasn't one of them. He suspected absentee, divorce, death, and even ditching when things got tough with her mom, but not that. "Well, he must have been a great man, because I'm looking at the proof."

Her cheeks turned so red they looked blistered. "Stop. I'm just me."

Yeah, and she was great. "Your mom was pretty hard on you growing up, huh? She scolded you back there in the room."

"Yeah, but it was because she loved me. She wanted me to be tough enough to stand on my own. She was hard on me, and sometimes it felt like I was never good enough." She got a faraway look in her eyes and then looked down at the table. "I don't think she ever considered that maybe I didn't want to stand on my own. I'm lonely. I have no friends. No family. No one to call if something happens. I go home at the end of the day to a dark house, and most of the time, I don't even turn the lights on because all I'm going to see is light shining on the emptiness."

His chest tightened. That was the perfect way to describe how he'd been living. Top floor penthouse or falling-down trailer, loneliness was loneliness. It meant no one was waiting for you at home. You were always cold, no matter how many blankets you piled on. It was hollow, aching, and breathtaking to sit down and realize there was no reason to go home.

She startled and slowly lifted her gaze. "I'm so sorry. I didn't mean to say all that. Forget I said it, please."

He swallowed the brick-sized lump in his throat. "I've felt it too. You just put it into words."

"I wish I could keep my mouth from running. I don't think and just say what pops in my head." She covered her face with her hands. "Just once, I'd like to not be a loser."

Tristan quickly switched seats. He took her face in his hand and made her look at him. "You aren't. You are beautiful, bright, funny, kind, and caring. I'm stopping there because the list of things that make you wonderful would take me all night. Your laughter, your smile, the way you see people, the way you see me—I've never felt more cared for. You punched someone because they were making fun of me. Everything about you is magical. You are a rarity. Anyone who can't see that is blind. You are more than good enough. You're great." Her lips parted, and he could see in her eyes that she was struggling with what he'd said.

"We probably should go, Tristan. Miami airport is super busy. I wouldn't want you to miss your flight."

He didn't want to go. Miami was warm, sunny, and there was Belle. "We could try."

She shook her head. "No."

And there it was. Two letters. One word. And it had so much power. He'd stopped short of telling her he loved her. If she didn't love or want him, it didn't matter how much he loved and wanted her. Saying it aloud, seeing the look of rejection in her eyes, would only make it hurt that much worse.

He put space between them and nodded. "All right."

CHAPTER 24

Telling Tristan no was the hardest thing Belle had ever done. Putting her mom in the nursing home, easy. It was best for her. Moving to Miami, easy. She needed to get away from Paul and have a new start. But looking into Tristan's brown eyes and telling him no crushed her.

She'd rather hear Laura telling her how pathetic she was than do that. Losing her career was easier. Belle loved him with all of her heart, and the one thing her mom taught her was that when you loved someone, you did what was best for them. He didn't need to be dealing with a hot mess like her. She could only imagine the write-ups in the papers if they were ever linked together.

He'd been quiet the entire ride to the airport,

keeping his eyes pinned on the scenery out his window. She'd hurt him, and she hated herself for it. There was nothing she could say to make it better. No words of comfort or parting wisdom. She was never going to love anyone like she loved him.

Man, Murphy's Law was getting its kicks tonight.

"You can take this exit and drop me off in the parking garage. That way you don't have to come in. I'm sure it's a madhouse in there." His voice was soft and lifeless. "I'll walk from there to the concourse."

"Okay." She did as he asked and found a spot as close as she could. "Tristan—"

"I know."

No, he didn't. She loved him, but if she said it, she'd never forgive herself. He'd be trapped with her. She couldn't do it. But she could show him. "I need to tell you something."

He opened the door and stepped out. "Please don't."

Belle hopped out of her side of the pickup and dashed around it to his side before he could shut his door. Lifting on her toes, she put her arms around his neck and whispered. "Please hear me."

She touched her lips to his and savored him. He had to hear her. He just had to.

He dropped his bag and put his arms around her.

She couldn't kiss him long enough or hard enough. There was no way to tell him how much she loved him. She wondered if he could hear her heart breaking. If he knew just how hard it was to love him enough to let him go. Tears threatened to spill, but she'd kiss him until he was deaf.

He broke the kiss and touched his forehead to hers. "I don't know what you were trying to say. I'm more confused now than I was before. I promised I wouldn't walk away from you again."

She stepped back and put a foot on the floorboard of the pickup. "You aren't walking away from me." Slipping onto the seat, she put her hand around the door handle. "I'm driving away from you, Tristan Stone." Then she shut the door.

Belle quickly shut the driver's side door and put the truck in drive. If he said anything, she wouldn't be able to leave. She didn't look back or shed a tear until she pulled into her driveway.

Then she laid her head on the steering wheel and cried the ugliest cry she'd ever cried. She'd let the only man she'd ever truly loved, leave. She'd given him up because he was wonderful. He needed someone who belonged in his world. Someone who would know what fork to use and when. Someone who had good taste in clothes. Hopefully, someone who saw him, who heard him when he didn't know what to say.

He needed someone, and that someone wasn't her.

TRISTAN STARED out the window of his private jet. Belle had just assumed he was flying out of Miami International Airport. Even after finding out who he was, it hadn't changed anything. Not the way she looked at him, talked to him, or kissed him.

She'd left him though. In an airport parking garage, gaping after her with his heart on the floor. He should have told her he loved her. What could she be thinking? Could she really be thinking she was a loser? That she didn't fit in his world? It was so far from the truth. How could she not see how beautiful she was?

He'd planned to tell her who he was after San Juan, but he'd chickened out. Simply being Tristan to her had felt good. But if she'd known, maybe he could've convinced her they could make it work. That she did fit. Perfectly. *Everything* about her fit perfectly, and without her, there was a gaping hole no one else would ever be able to fill.

For the first few hours, he'd tried calling her, only for it to go straight to voicemail. After the fifth message, begging her to call him back, he stopped calling. She wasn't going to answer his calls. He knew it deep down. She'd kissed him and then walked out of his life. Just like that.

He did understand how she felt that day in San Juan. Being left behind, not understanding what had happened, and not knowing if he'd ever be able to breathe again. He loved her. More than anything, he loved her. He didn't care where she lived, how she dressed, or where she worked. He loved her. She was the most amazing woman he'd ever met.

At some point he fell asleep, because as the plane touched down in Seattle, he was jolted awake. He didn't want to go home to an empty condo. He didn't want to turn the lights on and shine a light on the emptiness. He wanted Belle.

He went through the motions of getting off the plane, into the limo, and numbly taking the elevator to his penthouse. The sun was just coming up, and he felt like he'd been hit by a truck.

As he stepped off the private elevator into his living room, Grayson popped up off the couch. "Hey."

"What are you doing here?" he asked and shut the door. He dropped his things and walked to the couch.

"I had a feeling you'd need to talk." Grayson swung his feet onto the floor to make space for him.

Tristan folded onto the couch and kicked his shoes off. "It was a good feeling."

Grayson nodded. "Tell me about her."

He snorted. "I don't know if I can."

"Try."

Over the next hour, Tristan told him everything that had happened. From pretending to date her to watching her leave the Miami airport garage. Retelling it only made the ache in his chest seep deeper.

"You love her."

"More than anything or anyone in this world."

"So, go get her."

Tristan shook his head. "I can't. She doesn't want to be in a relationship. She has her mom there in a nursing home. It's not that simple."

Grayson gripped his shoulder. "And it's not that difficult. You have the money to do anything you want. Move a couple of mountains, do what you need to do, and make it work."

He raked his hand through his hair. "If she doesn't want to be in my world, I can't force her."

"Do you think she loves you?"

He'd been asking himself that question all night. "I don't know. I want to think so, but if she did, she wouldn't have just left."

"I don't know, buddy. I've been in a lot of things,

but I've never been in love." With a tight laugh, Grayson yawned and leaned back on the couch. "Maybe get some sleep, give her a little time, and see what happens."

Tristan stood. "Yeah, I think I'll take that advice." He yawned and gave Grayson a two-finger salute before sauntering off to his bedroom. He'd sleep on it and try calling tomorrow. Maybe she'd have had time to sleep on it too and she'd pick up.

Hope was all he had.

CHAPTER 25

*B*elle's phone rang, and she checked the number before answering. Tristan had called every day, sometimes three or four times a day, for two weeks. She wasn't going to answer him. If she did, she'd be on a plane and in Seattle, kissing him, before she could think it through.

At least it wasn't him this time. "Hey, Maritsa."

"You, one hour, my family's restaurant, no excuses."

It was a good thing she wasn't working her second job. Well, no, it wasn't. Business was slow at the diner. It meant no tips. "Sure."

"Don't worry about paying either. We'll do it family style again. Shawn and Ashley are coming too. He's flying in from California."

Belle smiled. "You two hit it off, huh?"

"That man makes me smile, laugh, and he loves my big booty. In my book, that makes him a keeper."

She laughed. "Those are great criteria, if you ask me."

"How about you and Mr. Tall Hotstuff? The way he looked at you, girl, he was in love with you."

The mention of Tristan sent her heart cratering. "He's back in Seattle."

"Seattle? And why ain't you there with him? I know you love him. You look at him with the same gooey eyes."

"It's not that simple."

"Don't talk no more. You fill me in tonight. My Yaya, she'll set you straight."

"Okay." Belle ended the call and dressed in something comfortable enough for Maritsa's Yaya to set her straight. Whatever that meant.

She headed out of the house and followed the directions she'd been given the first time she went to the restaurant. The place was packed, and she knew why. It smelled so good she salivated. She was going to scarf it with glee until the button on her pants popped off.

With the truck parked, she walked to the open front door. The very moment her foot hit the tile in the restaurant, Maritsa saw her and waved her over to a large table with at least twenty people gathered.

Belle hesitated. There were so many people, and she felt so nervous. The food smelled too good to abandon her plans, so she walked over and stopped at the only open spot. On one side, there was Ashley, and she waved and said, "Hi." On the other side, an older woman smiled and motioned for her to sit. The woman was round and weathered, but she had the warmest smile.

Maritsa and Shawn were across from her and canoodling harder than a couple in a Hallmark movie. "Hey! That's my Yaya."

Belle turned to the woman and sheepishly nodded. "Hi."

"I hear you have man trouble," the woman said.

"That's right. Yaya, they love each other, and she says it's complicated," Maritsa called from across the table. It wasn't possible everyone in Miami didn't hear her.

Her Yaya took Belle by the chin and turned her face one way and then the other. "You love this man?"

"I...it's not that simple. He lives in Seattle. I have obligations here. We're from two different worlds," Belle said as the woman trained her deep-set brown eyes on her. It felt like she was shoveling out anything in the way of her soul.

Yaya let her chin go. "You look me in the eyes and tell me about him. I'll tell you if it's meant to be and if it'll last."

What? Belle felt like she was at the fair, trying to stick a quarter in the fortune teller machine. "I…"

"You might as well do it. She won't take no for an answer," Maritsa said.

Ashley bumped her elbow. "She's not kidding. I swear, I feel like I've been run over."

Great. Now Murphy was working with Maritsa's Yaya. She wasn't going to get whammied; she was going to get trampled.

"You tell me. Go."

Belle lifted her gaze to Yaya's, and before she knew it, she was spilling her guts. "His name is Tristan Stone. He's sweet, kind, caring, loving. He saved my life. Someone threw me in the water, and he saved me from drowning. When he holds me, the world falls away and I feel safe. He's sensitive. He took care of his grandmother before she died. He does that, takes care of people. He's just wonderful, and I've never loved anyone like I love him."

Her Yaya nodded. "And?"

"I don't think I'm good enough. I don't know if I

can be who he needs me to be. He's a...billionaire. I'm working two jobs. He deserves...better."

The table had quieted while she was talking, and she could have crawled under it. Good grief. What was wrong with her?

"And who are you to tell someone who they should love? If he thinks you're good enough, isn't that enough?"

Belle blinked.

Yaya smiled and crossed her arms over her chest. "You go. You find him. You tell him you love him."

"But that won't change anything."

"You listen to Yaya. I'm never wrong, only late."

Find him and tell him she loved him? At least he'd know. He'd know she loved him, and she'd left him because she didn't want to be a noose around his neck. But he'd know, and that hurt look in his eyes might not haunt her anymore.

"Go." It felt like Yaya was giving her a command.

She shook her head. "He lives in Seattle. I don't have money for a plane ticket."

"I have so many frequent flyer miles that I'll never use them. I'll get you a ticket," Shawn said.

Maritsa grinned. "That's my man."

"I don't know where he lives."

Shawn smiled. "I bet I can find out. Him being a fan and all."

This couldn't be happening. Not to her. You didn't get second chances in life. Her mom had taught her that. Her life had taught her that. What if she told him she loved him and he didn't feel the same? "But…"

"You go. Trust Yaya." The woman stuffed her mouth with a pile of flavored rice and began humming. Apparently, Yaya had spoken, and the conversation was over.

"Okay." Did she just say that? What about her mom? She loved her, but she needed someone to hold her, kiss her, and love her. Being on the cruise with Tristan only highlighted how empty her life was. She loved her mom, but she loved him too. Families figured out things all the time. Maybe hers could too.

CHAPTER 26

*T*ristan rolled his shoulders and laid his head against the seat of his Maybach. Another day, another meeting, another call with no answer. He'd made up his mind earlier that he was done calling. After two weeks with no answer, it didn't take a genius to figure out it was over.

Grayson must have sensed how he was feeling, and he'd sent him home. He'd almost been pushy about it. Did he look that bad? He suspected he did. Lying awake at night, thinking about a woman, would do that do you.

He pulled his car into the garage and parked. All he felt was dread when he came home now. There was no one but him. It was cold, quiet, and empty. The views were great, but what was the point with no one to share them with.

Maybe he'd sell his penthouse and move. A change of scenery might be good for him. He got out of the car and stuffed one hand in his pocket and pushed the elevator button with the other.

The ride was quick, and he stepped into the living room of his home.

Belle stood in the room, less than ten feet from him. "What are you doing here? *How* did you get in here?" The number of questions pinging around his brain was making him dizzy.

"I flew in using Shawn's frequent flyer miles. He got in touch with your friend Grayson, and he brought me here." She chewed her bottom lip.

No wonder Grayson had nearly pushed him out of the office. The rat. "What are you doing here?"

She tugged on the hem of her t-shirt. "Um, I..."

"Belle, I've been calling you for two weeks. Why didn't you just pick up the phone?" He was too tired for games.

Her dark-green eyes held his. "This isn't something I wanted to tell you on the phone, and I wanted to see you."

"Then what?" He almost felt frustrated. Not almost. He was frustrated. She'd pushed him away, and now she was standing in the middle of his living room.

"I don't know if it matters. I don't know if it will change anything. Life doesn't give me second chances. Not when someone like you comes along. I'll understand if you don't feel the same way. Can't say it won't hurt, but it would be my fault since I walked away from you." She looked at the floor, and her shoulders sagged.

"What, Belle?"

She lifted her head, and her gaze locked with his. "I'm in love with you. Somewhere between fixing your hair, and kissing you on the beach in Amber Cove, I fell head over heels in love with you. Like I said, though, I'll understand if you don't feel the same way."

Belle loved him? Then why was she so insistent that they couldn't make it work? "But you kept telling me no. That it wouldn't work." His heart was racing so fast it was making his chest hurt.

"I wasn't exactly honest about what Laura said. She was actually cruel that day, which I should have expected. She told me who you were and then said I'd never fit in your world. I live in a shack, work two jobs, and take care of my...mindless mother. She said that I'd never be good enough for you." She hugged herself. "And in truth, I thought that too."

"You're more than good enough." He knew Laura had said something else. But not good enough for his lifestyle? There was no one better.

"I know. You showed me that. You treated me better than anyone ever treated me. In just nine days, you showed me I have worth. That I'm worthy to be loved and treated well. You showed me that love was more than words. That I don't have to settle for scraps. I'm so sorry I walked away. I will never do it again."

Before he said anything else or told her how he felt, he needed to come clean as to why he kept his identity a secret on the cruise. "I never told you who I am."

"I know."

"But you don't know why I did it."

She tilted her head. "Then why?"

"I just wanted to be Tristan for a little while. I was so used to being used that I just wanted a chance to blend in and be just one of the guys. Then I met you. You saw me when no one else did. I've never loved anyone the way I love you. Ever. I know I lied. I'm so sorry."

Belle smiled. "I don't care what your name is. I only care who you are. And I love who you are."

Tristan closed the distance, wrapped his arms around her, and lifted her off the floor. "You really love me?"

"More than I can say with words."

Belle was back and she loved him.

"Say it again. I want to make sure I wasn't hallucinating."

"I love you, Tristan Stone. I promise I will always see you and hear you. Even when you aren't using words." She held his face as she kissed him with the feathery, teasing kisses that drove him crazy.

He slid his hand into her hair and deepened the kiss, pouring every ounce of what he felt for her into it. If she could hear him, she'd know without a doubt he loved her.

Hours later, breathing hard from kissing and happier than he'd ever been in his life, he touched his forehead to hers. "I guess I need to do a little house hunting in Miami."

"Really?"

He pulled back. "If you think for one second I'm letting you get away, you're crazy."

"I'd actually considered handcuffs at one point." She slapped her hand over her mouth. "That didn't come out right."

"Depends on how you mean it."

Her cheeks turned fiery red. "Stop that." She ran her fingers through his hair and kissed his forehead. "I love you."

"I love you."

EPILOGUE

One year later...

Belle wasn't nervous or anxious. She was simply ready to stand on the Amber Cove sand and become Mrs. Tristan Stone. It was the perfect day, in the perfect place, with the perfect man. She was so happy she was floating on air.

Over the last year, her life had changed little by little. Tristan had moved to Miami while her mom was in the nursing home. They'd dated, and she'd fallen more in love with him, if that was possible. Then on Valentine's Day, he'd surprised her with a trip to Oahu, and he'd proposed. It was sweet, simple, and she'd said yes, a thousand times.

Her mother had declined rapidly, and she'd lost her

a few months ago. By the end, Belle was just glad she wasn't in pain anymore. After she died, Tristan and Belle had moved to Seattle, and Belle's two jobs had turned into one at a Seattle marketing firm.

Maritsa popped her head into the room of the chapel right off the beach. "I think it's showtime."

Belle grinned. Tristan had flown in Ashley, Maritsa, Shawn, and Maritsa's Yaya. Grayson and his Aunt Felicia were there as well. Somehow, she'd managed to piece together herself a little family.

She stepped out of the chapel into the mid-morning sun and immediately found Tristan. He looked incredible. Light-colored shorts, a short sleeve button-up, and that killer smile that made her weak in the knees.

Yaya turned and smiled at her like she'd won a ribbon for the prize heifer at a county fair. "I told you. You listen to Yaya, you do okay."

Belle laughed. She'd been right. Maybe a little gloating was in order.

The music played, her two bridesmaids walked ahead of her, and the world fell away as she stepped closer to Tristan. He was the love of her life. She couldn't imagine loving anyone else as much as she loved him.

"You look...incredible," he said as he took her hands in his.

"You do too."

The ceremony was short but full of meaning, with them promising to love each other no matter what storms they faced. Then the minister smiled and said, "You may now kiss the bride."

They kept it short and sweet, despite the temptation to make it anything but. Then the minister presented them to their friends and family as Mr. and Mrs. Tristan Stone.

Never in a million years would Belle have pictured herself on Amber Cove, marrying a great man and never being happier than she was at that moment.

Her mom was wrong. Life had given her a second chance, and she'd be forever grateful.

A Clean Fake Relationship Romance Book Two

The Bodyguard's Fake Marriage:
A Clean Fake Relationship Romance Book Three

The Matchmaker's Fake Marriage:
A Clean Fake Relationship Romance Book Four

The Beast's Fake Marriage:
A Clean Fake Relationship Romance Book Five

A Clean Army Ranger Romance Series:
The Ranger's Chance:
A Clean Army Ranger Romance Book One

The Ranger's Peace:
A Clean Army Ranger Romance Book Two

The Ranger's Heart:
A Clean Army Ranger Romance Book Three

The Ranger's Hope:
A Clean Army Ranger Romance Book Four

Clean Stand Alone Romances:

Love and Charity

The Mistletoe Game:

A Clean Christmas Novella

Bree Livingston lives in the West Texas Panhandle with her husband, children, and cats. She'd have a dog, but they took a vote and the cats won. Not in numbers, but attitude. They wouldn't even debate. They just leveled their little beady eyes at her and that was all it took for her to nix getting a dog. Her hobbies include...nothing because she writes all the time.

She loves carbs, but the love ends there. No, that's not true. The love usually winds up on her hips which is why she loves writing romance. The love in the pages of her books are sweet and clean, and they definitely don't add pounds when you step on the scale. Unless of course, you're actually holding a Kindle while you're weighing. Put the Kindle down and try again. Also, the cookie because that could be the problem too. She knows from experience.

Join her mailing list to be the first to find out

publishing news, contests, and more by going to her website at https://www.breelivingston.com.

facebook.com/BreeLivingstonWrites

twitter.com/BreeLivWrites

bookbub.com/authors/bree-livingston